PENGUIN METRO READS

ALL ABOARD!

Kiran Manral was a journalist before she quit to be full-time mommy. She was a blogger–columnist on gender issues for *Tehelka*, and her blogs were among India's top blogs. Her debut novel, *The Reluctant Detective*, was published by Westland in 2012, and her second novel, *Once upon a Crush*, was published by Leadstart in 2014. She is on the planning board of the Kumaon Literary Festival and on the advisory board of Literature Studio, Delhi.

PENGUIN METRO READS
ALL ABOARD!

Kiran Manral was a journalist before she quit to be full-time mommy. She was a blogger-columnist on gender issues for *Tehelka*, and her blogs were among India's top blogs. Her debut novel, *The Reluctant Detective*, was published by Westland in 2012, and her second novel, *Once upon a Crush*, was published by Leadstart in 2014. She is on the planning board of the Kumaon Literary Festival and on the advisory board of Literature Studio, Delhi.

ALL ABOARD!

KIRAN MANRAL

An imprint of Penguin Random House

PENGUIN METRO READS

USA | Canada | UK | Ireland | Australia
New Zealand | India | South Africa | China | Singapore

Penguin Metro Reads is part of the Penguin Random House group of companies whose addresses can be found at global.penguinrandomhouse.com

Published by Penguin Random House India Pvt. Ltd
4th Floor, Capital Tower 1, MG Road,
Gurugram 122 002, Haryana, India

First published in Penguin Metro Reads by Penguin Books India 2015

10 9 8 7 6 5 4 3 2

ISBN 9780143423577

Typeset in Bembo by Manipal Digital Systems, Manipal

Printed at Repro India Limited

www.penguin.co.in

To Kirit—

for being my 'love at first sight', 'knight in shining armour' and 'happily ever after'. Thank you for being the man I thought existed only in romance novels.

ONE

Rhea stood with her nose pressed to the porthole. The huge cruise liner she was on had pulled out of the port at Civitavecchia, near Rome, cutting through the crystal blue waters with ease. The huge, multistorey liner was to be her home for the next few weeks. As evening fell, the setting sun slanted its rays off the sparkling waters, riding on the horizon. She should have been elated—she was on a Western Mediterranean cruise, something she could have only dreamt about. But all she could feel was panic and the overwhelming sense of depression. Visions of scenes from movies like *Titanic*, *Poseidon* and *Life of Pi* flashed in front of her eyes and she had to do some quick deep breathing in order to calm herself down. *Everything is going to be fine!*

Boarding the ship that morning had been an experience grander than any film involving cruise liners and star-crossed lovers that Rhea had ever seen. She had remained open-mouthed ever since her first glimpse of the majestic liner docked modestly at the bustling port. As they entered the vessel up the ramp and took the elevator to the atrium, she was awestruck by the grandeur—curved staircases with gleaming wooden banisters, deep carpeted stairs and capsule elevators, tinkling crystal chandeliers and enveloping it all was the incredible buzz of thousands of people who were going to be together on this floating city for two weeks now. Almost fifteen-storeys high and with an army of staff bustling around to ensure that everything functioned the way it needed to, the Aqua Princess cut a swathe as it passed the smaller, more humble boats docked by the port as it headed out into clear sea.

As they entered, they were relieved of their carry-on luggage by the crew, and happily posed for the ship's photographer while drinking flutes of champagne served to them in welcome. Thereon they were directed to a lavish buffet until their luggage was delivered to their cabins.

It was tough not to smile when the music was pumping, people were dancing, and the social hosts roaming the premises to ensure everyone was having a good time during the sail away party. But now that they were back in the cabin and had finished settling their things into the rather compact, yet convenient, wardrobes, it was difficult to keep her mind off Samir. She sighed deeply.

'Rhea!' the voice cut sharply through the fog of her moroseness.

'Yes, Rina Maasi?' she replied instinctively, putting on her dutiful niece face and erasing the *Woe Is Me* expression that had pretty much become her default face ever since the rat, Samir, had bailed out on her days before their wedding.

Rhea winced at the memory of him leaving her behind to face the barrage of questions, and to deal with the dirty work of all the cancellations and refunds while he had hotfooted to Bali with someone he now claimed was the 'true love' of his life. Not to mention the non-refundables like the wedding trousseau that sat in her cupboard, mocking her. The gorgeous lehenga she had had custom-made in soft pink and silver . . . she had so looked forward to wearing it. Of course, after putting in all her savings—even if it was meagre—into buying her trousseau and into some of the wedding expenses, she was now also completely, totally, and absolutely broke.

'Come on now child, smile. Let me see those pearly teeth of yours, given I have none of my original set to admire.' Rhea laughed. When Rina Maasi commanded, you obeyed, even if you were her most preferred niece and could get away with disobeying her.

Rina Maasi was Rhea's mother's youngest sister. The 'eccentric one' amongst all the five sisters, she was Rhea's favourite aunt. The sisters had been known for their great beauty in their youth. From what Rhea had heard, it had led their father to apply for a pistol licence to chase off persistent admirers who had taken to loitering outside their residence.

'What do you think I should wear this evening?' Rina Maasi asked, drawing all the attention to herself. Rhea looked at her. She was a snappy dresser at the best of times and had outdone herself in honour of this cruise. They did have a dress code on board which aunt and niece had pored through before packing for the trip, so they had a few cocktail dresses, pant suits, skirts and smart blouses. The first evening on board hadn't been decreed formal, but Rina Maasi, she knew, would settle for nothing less than formal wear every evening. Spread on her bed in the tiny cabin without a balcony was a soft chiffon sari in pink, an indigo salwar kameez resplendent with patches of embroidery possibly meant to double as reflectors in case the ship was ever in danger of sinking and a blazing red formal trouser suit which was the least visually offensive of the lot, but which could clash with Rina Maasi's newly acquired copper hair colour.

'Surely, Maasi, you have other options which aren't as, err . . . as bright? What about the lovely *dhakai*s and *tussar*s you had in your wardrobe I last saw?'

Rina Maasi bristled visibly and fixed a beady, glaring eye through her spectacles on Rhea. 'I'm bored of them. I've decided to experiment with my look. I'm no longer a headmistress so I can stop dressing in muted colours and tasteful weaves now. Is there a rule that says once somebody crosses sixty she needs to drape her limbs in sack cloth and ashes?'

Rhea was forced to laugh. Rina Maasi was the brightest, cockiest, and chirpiest senior citizen she had ever encountered. And with her newly coloured, flaming red hair and post-box-red lipstick, she was quite a looker as well. She was also the original free spirit, having divorced her husband merely two years into non-blissful matrimony in the days when divorce was a social stigma, offering her scandalized family no reason other than, 'He bores me.'

'Pick the red then,' Rhea proffered generously. 'You'll make quite an impact.'

Rina Maasi picked the festive garment in question and held it against herself, looking into the mirror. 'Yes,' she said, nodding her head. 'This could be it. Not too sober for that cute silver-haired gentleman from two cabins down the passageway to think I'm an old fuddy-duddy who isn't up to a bit of mischief!'

Rhea rolled her eyes. They barely had twenty minutes to dress for dinner. She pulled out a slinky pewter dress that began off one shoulder and ended somewhere above her knees, bringing in the happy knowledge that she had legs which, as the cliché went, were never ending. It was a part of her trousseau. Or rather part of what would have been her trousseau had she married and been on her honeymoon right now. Not the kind of dress she normally preferred, being of the category who was more comfortable in denims and round-necked T-shirts, with the occasional jacket thrown on as a concession to formality when required. But she had a trousseau now and by Jove was she going to use it!

How Rhea ended up on this huge liner escorting Rina Maasi on a Western Mediterranean cruise was the stuff *Serendipity* was made of. It so happened that Rina Maasi had planned to go on a cruise after the wedding with her long time bridge partner, Sheela aunty. However, just days before they were to leave, Sheela aunty came down with a severe bout of dengue and was advised against travel and strain of any sort. When Rina Maasi wailed on and on about how she was going to be alone and how the cancellation charges would be like a double whammy, the family put their heads together and decided that Rhea, who needed a distraction from deep, dark, suicidal thoughts, would join her aunt on this cruise. Some swift string pulling later, a change of passenger details on the tickets and visas were procured by the travel agency head who was an old student of Maasi and had offered this cruise at a tempting discount.

At first Rhea refused point blank. But her family persisted and she gave in. As she looked at herself in the mirror, she was glad that she changed her mind. A freelance content editor who worked on a project-to-project basis, Rhea could hardly afford extravagances like a vacation aboard a luxury cruise liner. Her parents were retired educationists with modest savings, so there wasn't much to be passed on to their two children either, other than their love for the printed word and, of course, their DNA. As a person, Rhea could be persuaded easily and now that an opportunity of an all-expenses paid trip with a doting aunt presented itself, there was really no need for much pushing. They boarded the Air India flight out to Rome from the Indira Gandhi International Airport at Delhi and flew in companionable silence, while Rina Maasi caught up with her nap after downing a pill to help her deal with the inevitable panic attacks she dealt with while up in the air and Rhea contemplated life after being jilted practically at the *saat pheras*. It didn't help that they hit some turbulence mid route, which had a rather sombre kid sitting up front with his mother ask loudly if they were all going to crash and die.

She sighed again looking at her dress. When she had bought the outfit, Rhea imagined Samir helping her zip it up. Or help her undo it. Perhaps rip it off in a moment of passion! Not that ripping clothes off her body was part of his style. He was more of 'remove clothes carefully and hang them to air before getting down to nooky' kind of person.

But this was one of the things that she found attractive about him—he was always in control. A dull pain, like a blunt knife heated on a coal fire, stabbed her heart, again and again. This was perhaps the 300th time since the morning that she had thought of him. Samir Dasani. The man she had loved with all her heart and soul; the man she was going to marry and then sail into the sunset to live the happily ever after with. The man who was now so far away that he couldn't have heard her heart cry even if he wanted to . . .

Damn his perfect features. The soft curls that made themselves evident if he skipped a haircut, and his pink lips that got petulant at the smallest thing. His way of carrying himself into any room with the confidence of knowing that he would be one of the best looking men there. Damn the women who looked at him when she was with him, making her wonder if she had turned invisible for a moment! May he rot in a hell where they had no cricket on television! She cursed him in her head—may crab lice invade his pubes, may his intestines be infected with a particularly virulent strain of antibiotic resistant flesh eating bacteria. Tears welled up in her eyes again. *What kind of person breaks up an engagement ten days before the wedding over email?*

It struck her that perhaps she was better off without him but the very next moment panic would start setting in. She would be thirty in a couple of years from now and there was a good chance that she would end up the proverbial old maid—crocheting tea cozies, living with an army of cats and having little boys ring her doorbell and hide just for the fun of hearing her froth at the mouth and stomp her foot when she opened the door.

Rina Maasi noted the change in her expression and patted her matter-of-factly on the arm. 'Don't even begin the waterworks, girl. Just make sure you have the best time of your life on this cruise. That's your best revenge on that infernal idiot!' Maasi, God bless her, refused to refer to Samir in terms other than 'that infernal idiot'. In fact, Rhea seriously suspected there was no 'Suddenly Taken Ill with Dengue' bridge partner who was to be on the cruise with her, and that this was all a strategy to get her out of the city. After all, in the extended family of grim aunts, uncles and busy cousins, Rina Maasi was the only one Rhea got along with like the proverbial house on fire. If anyone could cheer and distract her, she could.

She wiped her eyes and got dressed under the watchful gaze of her aunt. Giving each other approving glances, they got out of the cabin and made their way towards the elevators. Suddenly a very tall, flustered man rushed past them, accidentally dashing into Rina Maasi with such force that she almost fell over. He seemed to be chasing a kid who had also brushed past them in great speed just seconds ago.

'Watch where you're going, young man!' Maasi said sharply, her voice rising just a notch, but one that could instantly quell a classroom of rioting pre-teens. The man stopped for a moment, looked back apologetically, and turned ahead to keep up with the knee-high tall, fleeing child cutting through the dinner crowd emerging from the cabins into the passageway.

He was, as Rhea noticed in one swift, all encompassing glance, rather handsome. An Asian, definitely, if not an Indian. It wasn't often that Rhea needed to tilt her head up to look at someone, and this person came close to needing a head tilt despite the four inch stilettos that she was teetering precariously on. When she did, she caught her breath. He was the kind of handsome that made it to the covers of romance novels, usually with muscles on display, and holding onto a swooning damsel with ripped bodice.

'I'm terribly sorry, ma'am,' he said in a voice that came from deep within the throat, looking disbelievingly at Rina Maasi who cut quite a dashing figure in tomato red, accentuated by a ferocious application of red lipstick, that could make those of a nervous disposition yelp and back away in fear. Rhea imagined she saw him wince as he took in the violent clashing hues of red that made up Maasi from head to toe. 'I hope I didn't hurt you. I need to chase down that little rascal before he gets into trouble or gets hurt.'

'You could have seriously injured my aunt!' Rhea said severely. 'What if she had fallen over and broken a bone or something? I hope you know that bones don't heal easily at this age. Just saying sorry wouldn't heal it.'

The man looked at her. His eyes were honey-brown and fringed with lashes so thick they needed to be outlawed in the masculine species. Rhea almost swooned.

'I am so sorry,' he said, looking at Rhea intensely. Their eyes locked and stayed for a few seconds, more than was the permissible limit for perfect strangers.

Rina Maasi coughed. 'Apology accepted, young man. Now be careful when running down corridors. I should have thought you've grown out of it by now.'

'Soni ma'am!' he gasped, calling Rina Maasi by the name her old students addressed her. Soni ma'am in turn cast a stern eye and examined him in detail from the top of his close cropped head to the soles of his very comfortable Tod's loafers.

'Kamal Shahani, headboy, from Earth house ma'am?' He introduced himself with the slight gush that adults have whenever confronted with school teachers from a distant childhood.

Rina Maasi threw a dramatic hand to her heart and cooed, 'Oooh, Kamal! Haven't you grown up! I couldn't recognize you. Fancy running into an ex-student here of all places, in the middle of the Mediterranean sea!'

Not such a surprise, perhaps, thought Rhea, given that an ex-student headed the travel agency that sold them this cruise and wrangled a fabulous discount, with freebies thrown in, for Rina Maasi from the operators. This he surely must have extended to this old boy from the school as well—not that this old boy looked like he needed any discount, going by the watch on his wrist, the loafers on his feet and the fine mother of pearl buttons on his loosely fitted linen shirt.

'Rhea, meet Kamal, one of the best students I've ever had the pleasure of teaching, and one of the best football players our school had ever produced. It was a pity he gave up sports for academia. The last I'd heard, you'd gone to an Ivy League university for your MBA?'

He nodded politely at Rhea, their gaze interlocked and held for all of an indecent five seconds before she broke eye contact. If felt like a physical wrenching when she looked away.

The person being investigated by Rhea's smoky eyes extended a firm, square hand, with nicely manicured fingers. His handshake was impersonal, but the warmth of his touch seared her fingers to the bone. Rhea had never felt such a reaction from anyone's touch. She felt herself melting to the bones.

'Pleased to meet you,' Kamal said, looking straight into her eyes. For a second, just a second, she thought his pupils dilated. It could also be a trick of the light. It didn't help that he looked like someone who'd just stepped off the fashion spread of a men's magazine and was the kind of delicious that would have had another girl, who wasn't mourning from being dumped at the altar, delighted to be making his acquaintance. Rhea was not accustomed to being in immediate proximity with attractive men. In fact she had an innate terror of them. She could feel her breath shortening and her tongue tripping on an appropriate, polite response, which resulted only in an impolite, amphibian sound emerging from her throat. 'Hello,' she croaked in reply, irate with herself for finding him so attractive.

He turned his attention back to Rina Maasi. 'Yes, ma'am, I founded a little start-up back in India. But . . . I need to excuse myself right now before that little rascal gets lost in the crowd. I will catch up with you the moment I get him back safely.'

He cast an unambiguously appreciative look at Rhea, smiled, and then scooted off after the pint-sized in short pants.

'You really need to watch your kid,' Rhea yelled after him in unconcealed irritation. 'He could hurt someone else before he hurts himself.' She did have a rather low tolerance threshold when it came to parents who couldn't make their children behave in public, and didn't hesitate to display her annoyance loud and often.

He stopped short a few paces away, and turned around. 'I'll keep that in mind, ma'am,' he replied in a low, sardonic drawl with the corner of his mouth turned up like he was laughing at a private joke. She bristled in annoyance at his manner more than his comment. The little one thankfully had been detained by a crew member in the distance and was being held hostage in readiness to be handed over.

'Men these days,' Rina Maasi said, shaking her head sadly. 'Have no time to appreciate a pretty young lady. Not a little start-up anymore though, the company he founded. From what I hear it had received some big buck infusions from venture capitalists. Quite admirable, to strike out on his own when he could have just joined his family in their trading empire. Ah, here he comes . . .'

She suddenly smiled, shifting her attention to the silver-haired gentleman from down the passageway who emerged from his cabin and politely inquired if they were staying on the same deck. Within seconds Rina Maasi was in an animated conversation, exchanging anecdotes and family tree details with him.

By the time Rhea extricated her aunt from the conversation and hurried her up to the dining room, the queue outside the main restaurant where they had reserved their table was startlingly long and it was already way past their reservation time of 8.30 p.m. All around them were flushed faces—either because of excitement or hunger, perhaps both. Despite the seasickness medication that she had self-administered, Rhea was still a trifle uneasy about downing solid nutrition. She could feel the beginnings of a migraine behind the right eye.

They ended up sharing the table with the dapper silver-haired gentleman, who turned out to be a retired Colonel settled in Chandigarh and here on the cruise with his son and his family.

They were way into their main course when Rina Maasi exclaimed again. 'Ah, there he is!' Rhea turned despite her best intentions and saw the right angle jawed one, now with a light jacket covering those broad shoulders, his hair slick and gleaming under the bright lights of the tinkling chandeliers and escorting a delicately pretty, if not hassled looking, petite woman, probably his wife, and two children. Rhea noticed that one of the kids was the runaway they had encountered earlier that evening.

She took a deep breath. All of five-foot, eight-inches, Rhea had a deep-seated envy of women who were tiny enough to be rescued in dangerous situations. She'd long learned to do her own rescuing, to be her own knight in shining armour and that she would never be swept away in anyone's arms.

'There is something so very appealing about a man in formal evening wear,' Rhea thought to herself, allowing for a moment, the grim, murderous thoughts of Samir to slide from her mind and make way for Kamal Shahani.

Kamal ventured to their table after seating the petite one and the accompanying kids at a table at the far end with a family who greeted them with a fair amount of bonhomie. He said his polite 'Hello, how are you' to Rhea, Rina Maasi and Colonel Singh. 'Ma'am, do join us at our table for dinner. Naina and the kids would be delighted to meet an old school teacher of mine,' he said. 'I'm sure I could have them join the tables.'

'I'm sure you would like to keep me away from that lovely lady lest I tell her all the stories about your school days and the trouble that you got into,' Rina Maasi said with a twinkle in her eye.

Kamal laughed. 'Her son is just as troublesome, so she knows that it runs in the family! And I've made it up to my parents for all the trouble that I caused them back then. In fact, I think I've made them rather proud of me.' Rhea marvelled at the matter-of-fact tone in which it was said and realized that she found the self-assurance very novel indeed. Most of the men she knew sought validation for their achievements, getting jittery if they felt threatened.

'But do join us, it would be lovely to catch up.'

At that moment, his eyes met hers and for the briefest of moments, there was a flicker of something familiar in them—a warm, molten longing. She had the overwhelming urge to stand up and put a hand to his cheek and check whether the cheekbones were as hard and unyielding as they looked or smooth and forgiving, and almost had to sit on her hands to keep herself from doing so.

Rhea looked across to where the two children and their rather pretty, young mother were seated. The live band was striking up some music which was still midway between migraine-inducing and foot-tapping.

'That's very kind of you,' she interjected swiftly, before Rina Maasi could get a word in, 'But I think we would rather join you some other night. It is the first night on board and I'm sure you would like to spend it with your family than being bogged down by old school stories.'

He shrugged, the extra broad shoulders beneath the jacket moving just a bit, 'As you please.' They exchanged cabin numbers and promised to catch up over the course of the days that they were on board this floating city.

He excused himself with a smile that softened his eyes just that little bit from brown to melted honey, when he looked warmly at Rina Maasi. 'It is so good to meet you again, ma'am, after all these years. You haven't changed a bit.' Rina Maasi smiled in the preening manner she had when her vanity was flattered. 'Tosh, you're still a right charmer, that hasn't changed too,' she replied.

He went back to his table, where Naina, with her pretty face and curvaceous, small body had been staring at them quizzically, an impatient frown creasing her brow. They had a quick conversation, post which she smiled politely and nodded in their direction when she caught Rhea's eyes still on them.

'Nice boy, filthy rich, very old money, lovely parents. I remember meeting them quite often. He had a younger sister too, I believe, she was at another girl's boarding school closer to Mumbai. I've never met her though,' said Rina Maasi. 'I heard he had not got married, but perhaps I heard wrong. Looking at the kids, he's definitely been married quite a few years now.' She picked up her napkin and placed it on her lap. Then she turned her attention to her plate and the retired Colonel who was now heartily talking about the combat zones he had been in. The Colonel's family, which comprised his son and daughter-in-law, listened politely, with the son occasionally interjecting to fill in details that his father may have missed.

The migraine was now pounding determinedly between Rhea's brows. It was like demons taking hammers and tongs to her eyeballs and the queasiness of the entire day on embryonic sea legs seemed to rush up to her throat. She excused herself from the table and rushed out to stand on the deck, in a quieter corner to breathe in some fresh air. As she turned the corner, she dashed into something solid, a chest with a familiar mother of pearl buttoned shirt.

'Whoa there, are you alright?' asked a deep voice. It was Kamal. 'You look a little unwell.'

'I'm so sorry,' she replied, feeling the bile beginning to settle from its precarious climb into her throat. 'I think it was just the noise and the crowd. I felt a migraine coming on.'

'You must watch where you're going,' he said, a slight smile playing on his lips. 'Thankfully, my bones are sturdy enough to take the impact.' She looked up and he winked at her playfully.

She blushed and realized he was still holding her at the shoulders, his fingers like little embers on her bare skin. Her heart was pounding in her chest. She hastily moved back, breaking the momentary contact between them. 'I'm so . . . sorry . . .' she spluttered, trying to hide the red warmth that she knew her cheeks now displayed. 'I should have been more careful!'

He smiled, looking down at her with eyes that seemed like they were searching for something. 'No problem. I had just gone back to the cabin to drop the kids off. It was way past their bedtime. They were dozing off at the table. Are you through with dinner already?'

'No,' she replied. 'I will go back in and join my aunt in a bit.'

'Hmm . . .' he said, and stood next to her, a strange silence between them. A silence that was comfortable, familiar.

'I get this strange feeling that we have met before,' he said. She froze. Of all the corny pick up lines a man could use, he chose this one. 'Damn and blast!' she thought to herself. Not another married man trying his luck with the first girl he sees the moment his wife's back is turned! Rhea had dealt with enough of them. She hadn't put him down for this, but then all men were the same, she told herself. Hadn't she just been jilted by one of the species?

'I'm sure we haven't!' she replied tartly. 'I would have definitely remembered you had we met before.'

A strange expression crossed his face. 'And so would I, I suppose . . .' he replied, thinking to himself.

'Damn! Why do all the best looking men have to be taken?' she thought, kicking herself on her shins mentally for replying without thinking. But Rhea knew that had they met before, she would have definitely remembered him.

'I . . . I have to go,' she said and he nodded. She quickly escaped into the inner confines of the dining hall where the presence of many people would hopefully break the sudden moment of forbidden intimacy that she realized had sprung up between them. An intimacy that was unbidden, uncontrollable and, she feared, unattainable.

TWO

The next morning dawned, bright and clear. The morning light rippled off the sea and cast sparkling reflections on the ceiling of Rhea's cabin. It was like a huge glittering light pattern.

Rina Maasi opened an eye, then another, and then shut both, groaning out loud.

'Good morning, Rina Maasi,' Rhea chirped. She had been sitting on the bed next to her aunt's, waiting for her to get up, and watching the light creep up to the ceiling and play its dance number.

She got another groan in response.

'Are you all right?' she asked, concerned.

'No, I'm not all right. I feel like someone took a sledge hammer to my legs and my knees have decided to lock themselves into position and not open up to allow me any pain-free movement!' Rina Maasi wailed. She unfortunately suffered from occasional, acute bouts of osteo-arthritic pain that rendered her immobile until the pain subsided.

'Aren't you going to even try to get out of bed?' Rhea asked. 'Can I help you, get you something?'

'Just my medicines, a glass of water, and call in for some breakfast, will you please? I'm staying put today. I think I quite overdid it in the excitement of yesterday.'

Rhea smiled sympathetically. And then she suddenly remembered. 'But we have a shore excursion today! Wouldn't you want to go?' It was their first stop—Naples. The city where the Neapolitan pizza originated, one with the ruins of Pompeii, the Amalfi coast and a UNESCO world heritage site. She had been reading her Lonely Planet and was most excited about actually being able to step into the ruins of Pompeii. And now it seemed she needed to stay back and play nurse to Rina Maasi who was playing the invalid to perfection, demanding everything from the television remote to a bottle of water to be placed a hand stretch away.

Rhea had signed up for the excursion with Rina Maasi, but now that she was sick, she didn't want to leave her and go off on her own. At the same time she felt sad about not being able to visit this much talked about city. She thought of the well-thumbed copy of Lonely Planet in her handbag with a quiver of unrequited anticipation.

'You go ahead without me, child,' Rina Maasi said, seeing her despairing expression. 'I'll be fine. Just need some rest and I'll be right as rain tomorrow.'

Being a school teacher did that to one, Rhea thought to herself, it made one speak in similes. She debated mentally. Maybe it was okay for her to go. This, after all, was a small cabin and she had all the help at hand. And it wasn't as if she couldn't call out. She would actually improve as the day grew warmer.

'Are you sure, Rina Maasi?' she asked, just to be sure. 'I could stay back. And you know how I dread going around alone with a group of strangers.'

It was not for nothing that Rhea had been awarded the title Shrinking Violet in her high school yearbook.

'You could stay with the Colonel and his family. Or better still, stick with Kamal and his family. They would be more your age and he will take good care of you,' Rina Maasi declared, not realizing that the last thing Rhea wanted right now was to be in immediate proximity with Kamal. Her limbs hadn't yet completely stopped trembling from that moment of physical contact between them. 'God, Rhea,' she chided herself, 'you are behaving like an adolescent! And this is a married man!'

'I'm an adult, Rina Maasi. I can take good care of myself, thank you very much!' she said with mock anger.

'I know *babu* . . .' Rina Masi said softly. 'Now go have breakfast. I forgot you were here to have fun leaving your sorrows behind and you will do just that.'

Giving her aunt a kiss and a hug, Rhea walked out to grab some breakfast. Unknown to herself, she cut a rather striking figure as she walked through the corridors to the dining hall. Long-limbed and a little lost, she walked towards the upper deck stairs. She was dressed in a pair of white linen pants, a bright green camisole and a light, cotton, white shirt. A pair of comfortable shoes, a woven raffia tote and a printed scarf tied to it completed her look. There was no make-up on her face—a perfect oval that was framed by her shining, black hair in natural waves—except for a slick of lip gloss that intensified the natural hue of her lips and her wheatish complexion and a gentle application of kohl in her eyes. She wore a raffia hat to keep off the sun.

As she climbed up from the lower docks to the one upstairs, Rhea was struck by the beautiful scenery. The azure sea stretched endlessly and in front was a Norman castle overlooking the port. There was a palace above the castle and a fortress, Castel Sant'Elmo, on top of the hillside, overlooking the bay. And beyond all these was the looming, sinister presence of Mount Vesuvius, now dormant. She took in a deep breath of the cool sea breeze, surveying what the city had to offer. Excitement filled within her to begin exploring as soon as possible.

She had forty-five minutes to herself before reporting time. She moved on to the ornate sky-lit café. It was already a riot with families and squealing children and honeymooning couples. And food. An enormous array of food was lined up in a semi-circle along the deck walls.

Rhea served herself at the buffet and found a table for two on the deck from where she looked out at the shoreline of the city they were to visit. 'Hello, good morning! Do you mind if I join you?' interrupted a deep, masculine, unfamiliar voice with a clipped British accent.

She looked up to see a rather buff-looking man, with twinkling blue eyes, the corners crumpled into a web of smile lines, looking down at her. She looked around. All the tables seemed to be taken. It would be impolite to refuse.

'Sure,' she replied with a smile. She turned her attention back to the Lonely Planet on her Kindle, researching the places they were to visit on their shore excursion. Rhea had always been a bookworm and her childhood was replete with anecdotes of how she had been found hiding in corners at family gatherings with her nose deep in a book. Not much had changed when she grew up, preferring the company of the printed word over that of human beings.

'Thank you,' he said and lowered himself into the chair opposite her. He plonked a big black coffee mug next to his plate. Rhea couldn't help noticing that his plate was a heart attack in the making—scrambled eggs, bacon, sausages, and all things fattening and laden with cholesterol were piled generously on it. A contrast to her muesli with cold milk and orange juice breakfast.

Deciding to be polite, she observed her intruder who was dressed casually in a pale yellow linen shirt and beige cargo trousers. His skin was tanned in an even manner that denoted either diligent application of suntan oil, or travels to places where suntan oil was the last thing on one's mind. Hair of the variety called dirty blonde spilled over to his shoulders. He was lean without being overtly muscular, and attractive in a strange way. He would have been in his late thirties, she thought, with the sun adding years and lines to his face.

'What is a pretty girl like you doing all alone on a cruise ship, if I may ask?'

Rhea laughed. She wasn't used to being hit on this quick into a conversation. 'Having breakfast,' she replied with a smile and a naughty twinkle in her eyes. He looked stunned by her answer for a second. She offered, 'Hi, I'm Rhea Khanna.'

'My name is John. I'm from London,' he said, cocking his head slightly with a big smile and offering a huge square-palmed hand. She put hers on it, as was expected. They shook hands perfunctorily. The contact was brief.

Rhea explained, 'I'm from Delhi. I'm here with my aunt, who unfortunately is a little unwell and resting right now, which is why I'm currently alone.'

'Good to meet you, Rhea,' he replied.

'Likewise,' she said.

'We seem to be the only two souls on our own in this restaurant,' he continued, looking around at the rest of the throng in the eatery.

'It is rather crowded,' she agreed, wondering when it would be polite to stop the small talk and concentrate on the food.

'I have a dislike for eating on my own, but I must get used to it.'

'Why is that?' Rhea asked.

'My wife just passed away a year ago,' he replied.

'Oh . . .'

His face, below the tan and the ruggedness, suddenly went tender. 'She had bone cancer. Unfortunately, we discovered it when it had reached the fourth stage. I'm starting my life all over again now. Learning to do things on my own, starting with going on vacations without her.'

'I'm so sorry to hear that.' She felt a sudden pang of pity and empathy for this complete stranger who was so open about his loss.

There was a minute of awkward silence when they both concentrated on the food. How terrible it must be, thought

Rhea, to lose a spouse to a terminal illness, and here she was, moping around like a month of Mondays because she had been jilted at the altar. It was a blow to her self-esteem for sure, but she would recover, she would move on. Moving on from something like a death of a loved spouse was something that seemed unimaginable.

She looked up at John who was now done with most of his meal and was preparing to fetch himself some more coffee.

'A refill of the orange juice for you?' he asked politely.

'No, thank you,' she replied, quite fascinated by his old world politeness, 'I'm done.' Samir would have gone off and got what he wanted to for himself without bothering to ask if she wanted something. She had put it down to him being a new-age man and she being a new-age woman. She didn't need doors to be opened for her, if that kind of chivalry still existed.

'Are you scheduled to go on shore?' he asked as he sat back, sipping from his refilled cup of caffeine.

'I am,' she replied, thinking this a good time as any to end the conversation. She stood up to leave. 'It was good to meet you, John. Have a lovely day.'

'Wait a minute,' he said hastily as she began moving away. 'Let's go ashore together. What excursion are you booked on?' She told him. As all good coincidences should be, they were on the same one. 'That's good. I'm lucky to have such pretty company. Shall we?' he asked, bending politely to let her go first.

He was laying it on with a shovel and she found it too amusing to take him seriously or take offence, as she would have, had it been someone else.

They made it off the ship to the bus barely moments before the bus was full up. As they clambered onto the bus, she spotted Kamal with his wife and kids tucked at the back. The kids had each grabbed a window seat, their nose pressed against the window in fascination of a new place. Only young children have such kind of fascination, she noted wistfully. Kamal smiled in brief acknowledgement, but soon got busy with the kids who were now pointing outside and asking questions.

Rhea turned her attention to John as they sat together. He was entertaining and a flattering companion, full of amusing anecdotes about his travels to what seemed to be every possible destination she ever wanted to visit and she lapped up his stories with interest. As they set off for Pompeii, they could see beautiful views of the city of Naples from the terraces of Posillipo. The bus wound carefully along the scenic coast road to Amalfi and the spectacular views had her craning her neck and fishing out her camera every second turn, where the bus politely halted to allow the passengers more photo ops than could be legal. The Mediterranean could be seen twinkling from the sheer drop at the edge of the winding coast road. Every now and then Rhea caught Kamal's eyes staring at her. And when she turned back she could feel two holes being bored by a very determined gaze. She tried to ignore it, but Kamal did not seem like a man who could be ignored.

They made a brief halt for lunch in Sorrento, at a local restaurant. Soon they were exploring the town on foot. John had been there before which made them cut off from the group and wander around on their own a bit. So much attention was flattering, it made Rhea giddy and giggly and she was only too aware of a pair of disapproving honey-brown eyes seeking her out from the crowd. It seemed every time she looked up, Kamal Shahani was staring at her. 'To hell with you, Kamal Shahani! I'm not going to be bothered by your indignant stares,' she muttered under her breath and then wondered why she was even bothering.

A short, but scenic drive later, they reached the ruins of Pompeii, where the guide painstakingly took them through the carefully preserved debris of what had once been a thriving city until that horrific moment when Mount Vesuvius rained down ash and lava, burying the city and its inhabitants in an instant. She was glad for the hat she had bunged on her head. It was a hot day and she found herself with damp patches under her arms as their guide took their group through the Forum, the Thermal Baths, Vetti's House and the Lupanare brothel, all buried by volcanic ash during the eruption.

Pompeii done with, the tour group returned to Naples for a tour of the city's landmarks, including stops at the Cathedral to visit the Treasure Chapel and S. Restituta Basilica which dated back to the fourth century. They were driven down to the Plebiscite square where they were shown the Royal Palace, the church of St Franceso di Paula, the Town Hall Square and the New Castle built by the French Family of Anjou.

The tour ended, but not before a stop at one of the oldest pizzerias of the city. It would be, after all, criminal not to taste the trademark delicacy of the place where pizza is reported to have originated.

Kamal and his wife were seated at a table nearby along with the kids who were in turn busy dismembering the pizzas that they were supposed to eat. Despite their mother's feeble admonishment about appropriate conduct in public, it was a mother of all messes on their table. She rolled her eyes apologetically when Rhea met her harassed gaze. 'These children,' she said across the tables in an attempt to explain in response to her disapproving looks, 'They're impossible to handle on holiday. I assure you they're better behaved back at home.'

Rhea smiled back in polite empathy. She had not one maternal bone in her body and these displays were quite enough to tempt her into getting her tubes tied while she still had the chance. Luckily, Samir hadn't been too keen on children—they had been well-matched in that sense. He probably considered her a perfect trophy wife, she thought. She was well read, carried herself with grace and confidence and knew how to work her way in from the soup spoon to the dessert spoon. To top it all, when she put her best foot forward she could give a room of grown men a crick in the neck from swirling their heads around to follow her movements. But then Samir wasn't part of her future anymore. A dark cloud of gloom settled itself on her head and began raining on her day. Her mood went from animated to morose faster than it would get a F1 car to accelerate to full throttle.

'Quite a handful, aren't they?' John said, looking at the kids indulgently. Rhea rolled her eyes. 'Not too fond of kids, are you?'

'Not really,' she confessed. She maintained a healthy distance from the under 10s.

'One of my biggest regrets was that we didn't have children. But now I realize that it was a blessing in disguise . . .'

his voice trailed off. Rhea hoped against hope that he was not going to dissolve into a fountain of tears because she was not up for sympathetic arm patting at the moment. But he politely excused himself to go the restroom. Rhea got up and walked to the exit of the pizzeria, waiting for him. She watched Kamal's wife as she hurried the kids to the restrooms too in the harassed manner patented by moms. Kamal strolled over to where she was the moment his family disappeared into the inner recesses of the restaurant.

'Hello,' he said, his tone concerned in a way it had no business being. 'Are you okay?'

'Why wouldn't I be okay?' she replied, bristling with a faint annoyance at the very proprietary air he was giving off. 'And why is it that every time I turn around, you seem to be watching me? Is something the matter?'

'Well, that depends on what you define something as,' he replied with a grave expression, and then broke into a half-smile, his eyes boring into hers, the gaze almost a probe. 'I just feel a little responsible for you,' he continued. 'Your aunt asked me to keep an eye on you during the trip when I dropped in to see her this morning to ask you both to join us for breakfast and the excursion. You had already left for breakfast by then. That's when she told me that I should look after you. And I tend to take my duties very seriously,' he said with a mock grin.

She bristled again, but didn't want to hold back. 'You know what, you can stop. My aunt is really sweet but she tends to forget that I am an adult who lives on her own, and am perfectly capable of taking care of myself. And if I needed looking after, it would definitely not be by you,

Mr Shahani. I think you have enough people to look after already,' she replied, gesturing towards the restroom.

His eyes narrowed slightly, anger flickering for a second. He looked even more handsome when he is angry, she thought weakly. But then, not wanting to give in, she gave him a scornful look, turned on her heel and stomped off towards where the bus was parked. What kind of hold did this man have on her? Why was she reacting so? She kept thinking as she walked angrily back to the bus. He was only doing what her aunt had asked him to, but why was she so affected by his mere gaze? Why was it that every time she saw him, she wanted to run her finger through his hair and touch his face? Why was it that she felt compelled to respond to him, to his gaze?

'Hey, hey, wait up!' It was John, who had just emerged from the restroom, hurtling after her. She smiled and stopped. He took her gently by the arm, and escorted her onto the bus. Her train of thoughts vanished, and she now settled in the bus once again, soaking in the scenery afresh.

It was all she could do to gather her flustered thoughts together and concentrate on the city and the sights she was trying to soak in. The conversation with John, which was nothing more than light banter, was amusing, but could not distract her from grim thoughts of dismembering Kamal for his unctuous, unwanted concern.

THREE

The next couple of days were going to be all at sea while the liner made its way around the 'tip of the boot' that comprised Italy, right up to the 'city of lovers' and canals and bridges and gondolas. Rhea couldn't wait to visit Venice, and was rather irked that it would take them a while of enforced camaraderie on the floating city before she could step down on solid land again. Her sea legs were still just that bit shaky, and only regular medication could help her hold her food down.

There was an insistent buzz on the doorbell to their cabin the next morning at the hour when breakfast had been done with and the mid-morning loomed ahead most emptily. Rhea opened the door and looked straight at Kamal. Her hackles, already prickly, rose further.

'Good morning,' he said politely.

'You?' She stepped back a bit as she stared right into the expanse of chest that lay visible through his v-neck T-shirt.

'Me,' he replied, boring his eyes through her till she felt uncomfortable in her deep pink vest and casual grey shorts which revealed more of her figure than she cared to.

'Lovely morning,' he said, in the idle tone of polite chatter.

'It definitely was, until this moment,' she replied defiantly. Rhea wouldn't let him have the satisfaction of thinking that his company was welcome to her. She also did not want him to forget how upset she had been with him staring at her all of the previous day.

He raised one eyebrow and gave her his infuriating half-smile. He didn't seem to think much of her comment and peeped in expectantly. Her heart skipped a beat as she inhaled the scent of his masculine perfume, though she pretended to be completely unaffected.

'Who is it, Rhea?' Rina Maasi called out from her perch near the porthole where she was downing her umpteenth cup of tea since the morning.

'Your ex-student,' Rhea replied, gesturing that he should step that way towards her aunt. Rina Maasi was craning her neck and patting her hair down to present a decent self.

Rhea tried to collect her thoughts into coherence. What was happening to her? She had been terribly rude to Kamal. But he was too handsome for his own good and seemed like he assumed that she would fall for him just like all the other women he must have encountered in the past. It was a good thing that when it came to married men, she was a girl with a firm moral compass, or else she would have been tempted to make him break his marital promises.

As he walked in, she watched his casual yet purposeful stride in a pair of flip flops and loose fitting white linen trousers that were rolled up to the ankles. His close-cropped hair was still damp from a shower. For a moment she felt an irresistible urge to run her fingers through his hair, right down to the nape of his neck . . . she almost groaned with pleasure.

'Did you say something?' he suddenly turned around and asked.

'Huh? No,' Rhea stammered. Her emotions were getting the better of her. She needed to keep them in check. 'No day dreaming around Kamal from now!' she reprimanded herself. But the very next minute her body tingled with the awareness of each of his movements and stance.

'Hello ma'am! I just dropped by to check if you were feeling better today and if you and your niece would like to join us for lunch,' he said sitting down on the single chair opposite her, making Rhea rather superfluous in the conversation. If anything, he was persistent. And polite. Not many students she could think of would repeatedly extend invites to meals to their ex-teachers.

'I must thank you for looking after Rhea yesterday,' Rina Maasi said. 'She told me you took good care of her all through the trip. It was really kind of you.'

Rhea gasped in shock. She had said nothing of the sort! In fact quite the contrary. She remembered ranting to her aunt about asking Kamal to keep an eye on her and the fact that he took it upon himself to keep not just one, but both eyes fixed on her. She would confront Rina Maasi on this straight-faced lie once they were alone in the room, she thought to herself. Kamal raised one cryptic eyebrow and tilted his head sardonically in Rhea's direction. 'Completely my pleasure, ma'am, although I don't think your niece needed much looking after. She was pretty well taken care of by her companion on the trip.'

Rhea, who had not yet told her aunt about having spent the entire afternoon on the shore excursion exclusively in the company of an unknown man, made frantic eye expressions at Kamal from behind her aunt's back, which he pretended to not notice.

'What companion?' Rina Maasi asked, a sudden infusion of sternness in her voice. She was, despite all her bohemianism, still a very strict aunt who was acutely aware of her responsibility in having brought Rhea along on this trip.

Kamal shrugged. 'Your niece has made some friends on the cruise. Am sure you'll meet them when you step out.'

Rina Maasi shot Rhea a look which indicated a full Spanish Inquisition was in the offing at the earliest convenient moment. Rhea dreaded these inquisitions by Rina Maasi. She had the art of asking the toughest questions without a hint of hesitation, polished by years of dealing with recalcitrant and defiant boys.

'Such a kind offer, dear boy, and how sweet of you to ask us to lunch. Unfortunately, I already have a lunch date, and must soon start getting dressed for it. As for Rhea, you must ask her if she wants to join you all for lunch. I have learnt not to speak for my niece, lest I get my head bitten off later.' She turned to Rhea and arched a brow; the vehemence with which Rhea had ticked her off the previous night had cut deep.

Kamal turned the full magnetism of his eyes on Rhea and she felt her knees turn unbecomingly into jelly of the version that had no business supporting the torso above it. Rina Maasi looked on curiously as the two of them were locked in a never ending gaze that neither wanted to break, until Rhea, with a great wrench of determination, turned her head away and looked out of the porthole at the sea.

'Would you join us for lunch, Rhea?' he asked. She turned to look back at him. Her name sounded vaguely erotic from his mouth. 'It would be a pleasure, unless, of course, you have other plans too.' His eyes were laughing. She didn't fancy being asked to lunch just because Rina Maasi had insisted he ask her himself and declined the offer straightaway.

'I have some things I must catch up with,' she said lightly, without the strength of her convictions, wondering if his pupils were perennially, visibly dilated, or whether it was something that just seemed to happen whenever she looked at him, 'Thank you for the offer though.'

He exhaled and stood up, passing within touching distance of her on his way out of the narrow passageway to the door of the cabin. She could have sworn the static electricity between them crackled so loud that it could have been mistaken for lightning strike by an unwary onlooker.

'Are you sure?' he asked again at the door, his eyes locking into hers. 'We could be quite amusing company.'

'I'm sure,' she replied, looking at him straight in the eye. If he thought he could drag her to lunch with his little family for his amusement, he was highly mistaken.

'Out of the cabin, boy,' Rina Maasi shooed Kamal, in much the manner she might have had when he was a gangling, pimply youth of fifteen. 'I have a date I have to dress up for.'

He laughed again, an easy rolling laugh that was mellow, warm, and comforting. 'Bye, ma'am,' he replied. 'Good to see you fine and back to your regular spirits.'

'I'll see you around Rhea,' he said in a low voice as he stepped out of their cabin and she stood at the door to see him off. She raised a defiant chin and did not deign to reply.

He laughed. Despite herself, Rhea felt a frisson of guilty excitement run up her spine.

With Rina Maasi dressed in her best dress and hat and off to an intimate lunch with the Colonel, to which Rhea was not invited, she decided to explore the facilities on the ship using the in-house newsletter as her guide. She put on a soft, flowing, yellow sun dress that tied halter style at the neck, comfortable canvas shoes, her huge floppy hat, and slapped on enough sunscreen to deflect skin damaging ultra violet radiation glinting off the lapping waves. When she emerged onto the promenade deck, it was full of people walking around in pairs or in groups, laughing, talking, or arguing. For a moment, just the briefest moment, she felt terribly resentful about being on her own in a cruise liner that was throbbing with people having fun together. It wasn't fair that Rina Maasi should be off on a date while she was condemned to ramble the vast ship on her own, trying to find a quiet corner to entertain herself! But she squashed that ungrateful thought down promptly.

Of course, had it not been for Rina Maasi and her generous offer to take her on this all-expenses paid trip, she would have been moping tears into buckets back in Delhi.

Her thoughts immediately went to Samir who deserved to be flayed alive and then hung from the branches of the nearest tree for carrion birds to feast on. Having indulged in bloodthirsty wishful thinking for all of two seconds, she firmly blinked back the fierce tears which were beginning to prick at the back of her eyeballs, and marched on through the layered decks, looking around for something to do. There was much to be done if one was the doing kind of person, which she realized she wasn't.

Perhaps she could sit in one of the all-day cafés and leaf through a book that she had in her bag—she always had a book in her bag, sometimes two. And there was, of course, the Kindle which she was now growing so attached to that she would soon need surgical separation to rid herself of it. Rhea was one of those nerdy girls who had grown up with a book somewhere in her bag. If not a book, she could be counted on to read anything printed that happened to be lying around—the label on a box of detergent or a bottle of pills, a menu card, a link someone tweeted, answers posted on Quora by random folk, anything. It was a habit that helped in emergencies, like the time when she was the only person to know the components of floor cleaner when a cousin, all of eighteen months, had ingested a bottle and needed his stomach washed out, and could tell the doctors what exactly it was that had entered his stomach.

After much wandering around through various levels of decks, Rhea realized that this could be the equivalent of a good cardio workout and was as bad as a day of mall hopping. She finally found a spot of shade on the Sky deck, under the awning of a café and with the view of the sea ahead, and plonked down. Pulling out her book and turning to the page that was bookmarked, she contemplated reading and having a bite for lunch together. Two pages into the first book of the very thick trilogy that she had carried along in the hope of finally completing it on the cruise, Rhea looked around to do some people watching—one of her favourite pastimes. Suddenly, she saw a familiar shadow fall across her table.

'And here I find you again,' said the deep honeyed voice she had turned down to have lunch with a few hours earlier. 'May I join you?' he asked, and without waiting for a reply, lowered his perfectly masculine frame into the chair opposite. Men seemed to be making a habit of this, joining her at her table, with a token 'May I?' Perhaps she should carry one of those inflatable dolls and place it in the chair opposite hers the next time she decided to sit by herself at a café. What was it about a woman sitting on her own that galvanizes those around to think that she needs company, Rhea wondered.

'I'm on my own for lunch since Naina's taken herself to the spa and will not emerge until the sun sets, and the kids are at the play zone, watching a movie and eating pizza. But I prefer not to eat alone on a holiday. So are we on?' he asked.

'I suppose,' she smiled with a sigh. She hadn't wanted to be alone too. And though his unsettling company was not what Rhea wanted, this time she let go of her resistance.

He quickly summoned a waiter and with quiet confidence, ordered a wine and dealt with the unpleasant task of placing the order for the entire meal as well. She watched him take charge and for some reason immediately compared the situation to when she and Samir were together. 'Why don't you order till I reach,' was what he would say every time they had to meet. This was supposed to compensate for his delay.

'So tell me, why would you be accompanying your aunt on a Mediterranean cruise?' he asked. 'I'm sure you have company your age who you would prefer to be with.'

'Well, the first reason is that she's paying for my trip. And second, and more importantly, she's great fun to be with.'

'Ah,' he said, looking at her with an expression that was soft, intrigued, and probing. 'That explains a lot.'

'What does it explain?' she asked, curious.

'The fact that you are so different from most other women on this ship. You don't have that seen-it-all, done-it-all, jaded look these veteran travellers have; you would rather stop and gaze at a beautiful view than take your phone out and go click click click to Facebook or Instagram it at that very moment.'

She laughed. 'I'm not a very social media kind of person.' She paused. 'In fact, I'm not a very social person to begin with.'

'I saw that yesterday. You were so prickly with me when all I was doing was trying to ensure that you were okay. That is what makes you different and so much more fascinating,' he replied, his face dead serious. Had anyone else said it, the line would have sounded corny. But somehow, coming from him, it felt like it came straight from the heart, or the gut, or wherever sincere lines are supposed to come from.

Rhea felt her face burn to what was definitely a red that only a sunburn could rival. She tried to hide her embarrassment by quickly turning her face away and concentrating on the blue expanse around them. She sighed. She was suddenly reminded that she could have been on her honeymoon right now, but instead she was on this cruise liner, somewhere in the midst of the Mediterranean, with the blue sky above and cottony clouds floating lazily across it. The sea whooshed below them, noisier than she had thought it would be. She smiled at Kamal. He was giving her a long, searching look, as if trying to figure what she was thinking. Why had Samir never cast her such a look? Perhaps because he was always too busy giving his phone or his laptop those long, yearning looks. And perhaps on that phone or on that laptop was the curvaceous one, now hanging onto his arm at a beach in Bali, for all their common Facebook friends to see and snicker about it behind her back. Oh the humiliation! She would deal with that later, once she was done with burying the hurt.

'Now for the real reason you're on this trip . . .' he began. 'Wouldn't you rather have spent the trip with someone else, a friend perhaps?'

Was this his way of asking about her romantic status right now? She narrowed her eyes, not realizing that the reflection of the sky in them made them sparkle in the most alluring manner. She gulped down the rest of the wine in her glass, feeling it surge through her blood stream. She took a deep breath and went ahead with the story she was sure she would never be able to tell in regular circumstances. And that too to a complete stranger.

'I was to be married. I would have been on my honeymoon right now,' she said, egged on by some strange urgency to lay it all bare. She manoeuvred some fettuccine around her fork and navigated it to her mouth.

He raised an eyebrow, expecting her to continue.

'Do you really want to know all this, or are you just making polite conversation?'

'I'm not just making polite conversation, I hate making polite conversation,' he replied.

'Well, that makes two of us then.'

His eyes narrowed down to slits. 'So, what happened?'

'He ditched me. Via email, the bastard!' she said, choking on her words, jagged and raw, as the hurt she had battered down all these days rose up her throat. 'He ran off to Bali with another woman and sent me an email telling me the wedding was off. Ten days before the wedding. He didn't even have the courage to take my calls. I had to tell everyone that the wedding was off. It was the most devastating experience of my life.'

There was a long silence at the table. She poured the rest of the contents of the wine glass down her throat hurriedly. The waiter had barely refilled the glass than she touched the stem again and drained it to the last drop in one defiant gulp.

'Nice wine,' she said, filling the void of silence between them. He smiled and nodded his head, then went back to being grim and concerned.

'I cannot imagine someone leaving you for another woman,' Kamal said. 'He must have been an idiot.' She could see a small spark of anger in his eyes and a tightening of the jaw.

'All men are idiots,' she replied, letting the wine give her the courage that she did not normally possess to state her unstinted opinion. 'All men are cads and lowlifes and cheaters.' She ranted a bit more about how men were one level above primordial swamp creatures, unmindful of the fact that one of the specimens was seated right across her. She didn't know why she was venting like a child but she didn't care, the wine had made her a bit reckless too.

He smiled and looked at her with a frank, assessing gaze, 'We may be. But you are pretty much perfect, perhaps that scared him off.'

The directness of the statement knocked the winds out of her sails. She felt like she had been head butted in the solar plexus. Rhea went quiet, unsure where the conversation was headed.

He looked at her for a long, never ending moment. Her knees quavered unseemingly. She gulped, wondering what was coming next.

'Don't be flattered,' she told herself sternly, 'that's what they do, these men, they flatter you so much so that you fall into their arms willingly. You don't want to be the next scratch to his seven year itch, do you?' She sat up straight in her chair. The two glasses of wine she had had made her wilt a bit.

'I hate all men,' she said, frowning with the effort to focus on him and her words together. 'I hate men. We should just stick to girlfriends. I love my girlfriends . . .' she slurred.

Then a sudden realization, 'Not like that, I mean, not in a sexual way, you know . . . oh my god, not in that way, I mean I have friends who are gay and I love them but not in that way . . .' She threw a hand out dramatically, in an extravagant gesture to emphasize her point and noted in some distant corner of her mind that she was definitely drunk. Then, with horrified eyes, she saw in what seemed like time lapse photography, her hand striking his glass and red wine spilling over his white linen trousers. More specifically, the crotch area of his white linen trousers. He stood up with a start. The area at the crotch of his pants was red—an unwary onlooker would imagine a scary encounter with sharp objects. 'Mother earth swallow me now and do not burp up my remains! He's going to kill me!' were her first thoughts.

'I'm so, so sorry,' she said, picking up the table napkin and trying, ineffectively, to dab away the red stain before realizing it was located at a very controversial spot. Dabbing at that spot in public would lead to complications she did not want to contemplate, and the handful of diners at the café were already looking at them curiously. So she stood still, or as still as she could manage, and continued apologizing on a loop, realizing that perhaps she had drunk a little more of the fine red wine than she should have, and needed will power and firm support to stop herself from swaying to the rhythm of an unknown music that wasn't more than the dip and swell of the sea beneath them.

He brushed aside her apologies with an amused laugh, 'Don't worry, these are old pants and I was thinking of discarding them anyway.'

'But . . .' she swayed a bit as she tried not to stare at the stained area.

'Are you okay?' he looked at her with concern as he signed the bill he had called for. Then she felt him move forward and take her in his arms, trying to steady her. For a moment their eyes met. 'God, woman!' he groaned as he brushed a stray strand of hair from her forehead. 'We need to leave. I'll take you to your cabin.' She nodded, electricity passing through her as she inhaled his perfume. He moved away a bit, took her gently by the elbow, and steered her towards the elevator.

The two went down the levels to her deck where he took the card from her, swiped the door open, and led her gently to the bed and lay her down. She went unresistingly. Some unfettered part of her wanted to close her eyes and put her arms around him, but her eyes closed on their own and her arms fell like lead on her side. She could feel determined hands pulling off her shoes, putting her legs up on the bed and drawing the blanket over her. 'I hope that bastard who brought you such distress writhes in hell,' he whispered, his hand stroking her hair. Rhea felt a delicious arousal spread through her, and she pulled him to herself, his eyes probing hers. She lifted her face to be kissed.

'I can't . . .' he said, pushing her back to the bed gently. 'You need to sleep it off.'

She wanted to ask why, but a second later, she heard the click of the door shutting behind him. Rhea had a sudden feeling of being abandoned. Kamal was very different from all the men she had known in the past—the gentle and dreamy Shaukat of the documentary film making agency who needed a puff or two of weed to calm himself before love making, the hedonistic Raj of the TV commercial production house who could party all night till his eyes were pinpricks and yet be raring for more and finally, Samir, busy, important, self-obsessed, with the urgency of the corporate world clinging to him even when he was supposed to be with her.

Kamal was different from them all, and he had rejected her. Thankfully for her, sleep took over before she could begin analysing the mixed emotions of attraction and disappointment.

FOUR

Rhea went into a deep sleep, oblivious to when Rina Masi came back and looked over her worriedly. Kamal had already told her that Rhea had fallen ill, had taken a pill, and therefore would be sleeping for a while. She ordered in dinner for two and waited for her niece to wake up.

When she finally awoke, her concerned aunt ordered her to keep lying down and gave her some soup. For some reason Rhea was able to go right back to sleep after that, and got up bright and fresh the next morning. As she freshened up, memory of the previous evening hit her like a bolt. She remembered the wine spilling, Kamal's gentleness, him helping her back to the cabin, the urge to kiss him, and his turning away. She felt a deep sense of embarrassment as she recalled him pushing her away.

'I haven't really explored the ship,' Rina Maasi declared before the breakfast settled in in her stomach. 'Let's spend the day wandering all over the ship. My knees are in better shape too, and might just cooperate. Show me all that you've discovered on it.'

Rhea had been in a dazed mood and her aunt seemed determined to jolt her out of it.

They began by wandering the various levels of decks that Rhea had already explored in the time she had had to herself. Just then Rina Maasi spotted the shopping arcade and the atrium. Like any self-respecting woman born with the dominant shopping gene, she squealed in delight and took an immediate detour into the arcade.

Rhea followed meekly, knowing that she could only look and lust, not purchase, given that her bank account was already pipping alarmingly with alerts about dangerously low credit balance.

'Stop moping around like a month of Mondays,' Rina Maasi commanded Rhea, dragging her by the arm into a store selling exquisite diamond jewellery, 'Just enjoy the moment!'

While Rina Maasi tried on some rings and earrings with an open-mouthed inspection of her reflection in the mirror, a familiar voice piped up loud from the counter a turn away, hidden from plain view. 'I want these, Kamal,' Naina's voice was clear and petulant. 'It's been so long since you've bought me any jewellery, just this pair of diamond earrings and I promise I won't badger you about any of your girlfriends ever.'

Rhea gasped. She had heard of open marriages in the middle class world that she was a part of, but hearing about it with her own two ears was a shock by itself. Rina Maasi was distracted to madness by a tennis bracelet she was trying on, pulling out her phone, putting her reading glasses on and doing complicated conversions into Indian rupee to figure out if she wanted to buy it. 'So what if I don't play tennis,' she rationalized with her practical self, 'It's beautiful and I can always justify the purchase by willing it to you when I die.' She looked at Rhea with a big exaggerated wink. 'Don't bump me off on the cruise to get your hands on it, though.'

'Don't be silly, Rina Maasi, it would take more than a tennis bracelet to get me to push you overboard. Now if you add your *kundan* and *polki* set to the bargain, I just might.'

They laughed. Rina Maasi put the coveted bracelet down on the velvet tray with great reluctance and stared at it lustfully.

'Should I pack it for you, madam?' the smiling girl behind the counter asked.

Rina Maasi sighed, and reached a hand out to touch it again.

'Give me a minute, let me decide . . .'

'Good morning! I thought I heard you!' Naina chirped, coming out from the other end of the store. Her ears were twinkling with what could have only been the newly acquired diamond studs she had been badgering Kamal to buy her. He was at the payment counter, forking out his credit card and looking most dapper in a white shirt over fitted blue jeans. 'Look at what I managed to wheedle out of Kamal this morning!' she said, the excitement of a new purchase evident in her voice. They oohed and aahed over it as mandated, and Kamal sauntered across, greeting them politely. He then handed the bill to Naina with strict instructions about keeping it safe and that he hoped she knew that he would not do the running around required to get a duplicate bill once they were back in India.

'It should be declared hazardous to the health of one's wallet to accompany a woman into a jewellery store,' he said wryly. 'Naina never lets me leave without buying her something. I should have learnt it by now.'

'But that's what is so lovely about you,' Naina replied, standing on her toes and pecking him chastely on his cheek, 'You never learn.'

He shrugged, looking at Naina affectionately. 'Don't bet on it. I'm not accompanying you into any store ever again for the rest of our lives.'

She hugged him again.

'So,' Kamal's eyes sought Rhea's out and settled on them, like an errant piece of a jigsaw puzzle finding its locking piece, 'Bought anything?' He seemed to be determined not to mention the previous day for which Rhea was grateful.

'I might just buy this bracelet,' Rina Maasi replied, still caressing the strand of single diamonds in a frisson of indecision. 'And Rhea wants to buy a ring, but she won't let me buy it for her.'

Rhea stared back at him, jutting her chin out determinedly. 'No way Maasi. I prefer buying my own jewellery. And I don't take guilt gifts.'

Guilt gift, she told herself. That was what he had given Naina, a gift for her to hold her peace while he philandered around. She stared at Kamal with her eyes narrowed.

He raised one eyebrow quizzically, and cocked his head. Rhea felt a huge urge to rush and kiss him, but she controlled herself and turned her attention to Naina and Rina Maasi who were discussing diamonds and caratages. Soon the purchases were packed to be taken, they said their goodbyes and promised to meet soon for a meal.

'Such a generous boy,' Rina Maasi said as they went their different ways. 'He was the same in school. Would give away his tuck to everyone and then be without tuck himself until the next batch of stock arrived with his parents.'

They settled down for lunch at one of the cafés on the deck. As they were half-way through their aperitifs, John came up to the table. Rhea hastily made the introductions.

'Rhea didn't mention that her aunt was such a classic beauty. Now I know where she gets her good looks from,' John said, taking Rina Maasi's hand to his lips and kissing it reverentially. 'It's a pleasure to meet you, ma'am.'

Rina Maasi melted immediately and thanked him. She never stopped smiling after that.

'And you are just the person I was looking for,' he said turning towards Rhea and smiling down at her. 'Would you care to join me for the Broadway show tonight?'

Rhea looked uncertainly at Rina Maasi.

'Oh go right ahead!' she said graciously. 'Don't worry about me, I have plans for dinner with the Colonel anyway!'

Hmmph. It was rather unfair that her aunt who had three decades on her seemed to have a much more happening social life than she did!

'I would be delighted to,' Rhea replied. They agreed on a time and venue to meet up before the show and parted ways, but not before John kissing Maasi's hand again in a charmingly exaggerated, old-fashioned manner that got her chortling with laughter and rapping him on his shoulder with her napkin.

'So, how is it that you did not mention you spent all day with this delightful man on the shore excursion?' Rina Maasi asked, her brows knitting themselves into a query. 'Tell me more about him. He must be pretty interesting if you spent the entire day with him.'

'Ah, there's nothing to tell, really, Maasi. We met at breakfast that morning, and since we were both going on the excursion alone, we sort of paired up.'

'Now isn't that cute,' Rina Maasi said, giving a piercingly investigative gaze at Rhea and trying to read the inscrutable expression that she had promptly plastered on. 'So is this the person Kamal was saying had kept you entertained through the shore excursion?'

Rhea nodded.

'He does seem to be rather old, though, doesn't he?'

'Tell me about dinner with the Colonel,' Rhea asked, trying to move away from the topic. 'You seem to be getting rather fond of him.'

Only too delighted to have the topic of conversation turned right back at her, the older lady's face softened. 'Isn't Bikram adorable? I wish I had met him some forty years ago. But then . . .' she trailed off, and then squared her narrow shoulders determinedly, 'It's never too late, isn't it?' They chatted some more as they walked to their cabin.

Colonel Singh arrived at their door at the dot of 20:30 hours, as decreed, to pick up Rina Maasi. She was, as usual, putting the finishing touches to her hair. He regaled the two ladies with tales of hand-to-hand combat on the eastern borders of India, and living in tents in sub-zero temperatures when they had to melt snow to drinking water, and how their whiskers and toes froze, until Rina Maasi had to gently dissuade him from continuing with his gruesome stories for fear of ruining her appetite. After they left, Rhea bagged the mirror to get dressed. She slid into a sheath gown in a wonderful bronze that clung on to her at all the right places and dipped a bit at all the wrong ones.

As she waited for John to join her outside the main theatre where the show was to be held, she noticed Kamal and Naina walk in. As the huge doors swung open smoothly, almost obsequiously, Rhea stared at his long frame, his ease and stylishness and the care with which he ushered Naina in. She felt a familiar tug at her heart and hoped her own escort would arrive soon. John arrived looking a little rushed, still buttoning the cuffs on his shirt with the studs, his dinner jacket in hand, and his hair damp from a recent shower. He smelt fresh and had taken the trouble to run the razor on his cheeks for tonight; she was glad the bristly stubble that had accompanied him earlier was not in evidence anymore.

'I'm terribly sorry,' he apologized, sweeping in and gathering her in an embrace that she wasn't sure she quite appreciated yet. She disentangled herself and moved pointedly towards the theatre. 'Shouldn't we go in?' she asked. 'It sounds like they're starting.'

As the doors swung open, some muted applause filtered through.

'Mmm,' he said, swaying alarmingly close to her, 'You smell good.'

'Thank you,' Rhea replied blithely, noting an alarming hickey on his nape that his shirt's collar could not hide. Well, it was either a love bite or he was breaking out in hives, or something contagious. She wondered if it was appropriate to be at necking distance with him. Spending her trip dabbing calamine lotion to contain an itching outbreak on her body was not her idea of fun.

As she lowered herself down into the confines of the chair, Rhea realized they had picked seats right next to Kamal and Naina. Kamal smiled and rose politely. Quick introductions were made and the men shook hands in the testosterone fuelled manner that indicated they were testing how far they could go without snapping the other's wrist off.

'Where are the children?' Rhea asked Naina, more out of politeness than genuine curiosity.

'There's a magic show at the kids' zone and we have hired a babysitter to put them to bed after that. So, hopefully, I can go dancing after this. Though I must find myself a better dance partner! Kamal has two left feet and dance moves that went out with Travolta.'

What was that they said about men who danced well, Rhea was tempted to add, but decided against it, given it was absolutely none of her business. Naina was a delicate beauty, with a fine bone structure that made her face a millimetre away from looking pinched and wan. But there was sadness in her eyes that Rhea could only begin to wonder about. The sparkle of the morning's purchase had dissipated. Kamal was gentle with her, even caring, but there was no chemistry between the two. Just some strange dynamics, which, to Rhea's untrained eye, seemed more fraternal than marital. Was this what happened after marriage and a couple of children, she wondered? Did the spark completely fizzle out and morph into a sanitized version of friends with benefits? She thought of her own chemistry with him and felt uncomfortable.

The lights dimmed and the music struck up a din that made further conversation impossible. The drums rolled, the curtains went up, and the dancers swanned out. It was completely a novel experience for Rhea—the spectacle, the dancing, the live singing. She sat beguiled, leaning forward in her seat, realizing that this was her real life equivalent to watching a show on Broadway. Feeling a pair of eyes on her, she looked to her right and spotted, in the faint light, Kamal staring at her with an intrigued expression. He kept looking, unapologetic about being caught staring. She felt her heart lurch violently within the chest cavity and gripped at the seat's armrests to steady herself. She swept a shaking hand along her forehead.

'Are you feeling all right?' John asked, his eyes narrowing in, what seemed like, concern.

'I think I'm feeling a little unwell,' she confessed; anything to get away from the close proximity of Kamal, never mind that he was two seats away and one of those seated his wife.

'Let's ditch this gig,' he whispered back in her ear, and rose, escorting her out of the theatre with an apologetic wave to their newfound acquaintances in the adjoining seats. She quickly walked out of the doors, trying to quell the uneasiness rising within her. It wasn't becoming to lust after a married man. And it was not appropriate for a married man to give her such an open cause to lust after him, that too in the immediate presence of his wife. She was glad to get away from it all.

They went to a restaurant on the deck where they had a quick dinner, while John's attention grew more amorous. Rhea realized it was time to call for an end to the whole thing.

'It's been a lovely evening, John, but I'm tired now, and want to go to bed.'

As the words left her mouth, Rhea realized that she could have framed the sentence better, in a non-ambiguous way, given that John had risen from his chair, swiped his card, and taken her arm to lead her to the elevators.

She didn't realize until they were in the elevator going down towards the cabins that they were headed someplace definite. John seemed to have something in mind as he stood too close to her for comfort.

'I think we're on the wrong deck,' she protested, as he steered her down the passageway.

'We're going to my cabin where I will offer you some excellent wine I have brought with me onboard and then we can chat for a bit. Is that okay?'

She nodded. Perhaps all he really wanted was to chat. She was grown-up enough to handle things if they went another way.

They entered his cabin and he let her in with a flourish. 'Wow! I'm impressed!' Rhea exclaimed, as she scanned what was certainly a more expensive room with a fantastic view of the deck and the sky. The furnishings were expensively done in grey and blue, very different from their functional one. John pulled out a bottle of wine from his mini bar and two glasses and poured some for each. Rhea wanted to say no, considering how she had reacted the previous day to just a few glasses of wine, but felt it would be rude.

They sipped their wine in companionable silence when John suddenly asked, 'So, tell me about yourself. How is it that someone like you is single? Or do you have a boyfriend waiting back at home?'

'No, no boyfriend,' Rhea said with a smile. She felt a bit uncomfortable, considering they were completely alone.

'Really? Don't you get lonely?'

'Yes and no. John I really must be going. My aunt . . .'

The conversation was taking, what they call, an uncomfortable turn.

John suddenly got up and stood next to her. He pulled her up and drew her towards him, his arms on her shoulders and his lips on hers, gently exploring her mouth with his tongue. Rhea was too shocked to react. She should have seen this coming, she realized. Perhaps she had led him on. But as she tried pushing him away, to her horror, John pulled her dress down her shoulders and carefully planted kisses where only few men had gone before. Her dress slipped to her feet and she stood in his arms, feeling quite exposed in her lacy number which barely covered her essentials. John took it as a sign and put his hands in the small of her back, pulled her closer. 'Oh Rhea, I've been wanting to do this since I saw you . . .' he said, getting a bit more frenzied, and now kissing her deeply on her lips.

'No, John, no!' she managed to say aloud, and pushed him away gently. Then as he watched confused, she pulled her dress back up.

'What happened?' he asked.

'I'm sorry,' she said, still struggling with the dress, which had, in all manner of things lycra-enhanced stubbornly refused to unravel quickly and allow her to regain her modesty.

'It's me . . . I'm just not ready for this.'

He pulled back from her, his eyes heavy, his breathing ragged, and stood against the wall—hands in his pockets, jacket and shirt off and his hair mussed up from when, she realized, her hands had clutched it in momentary abandonment.

She opened the door. 'I'm sorry John. I'm sorry if it seemed like I was leading you on, but . . .' she said softly as she rushed out, 'I can't . . .' She could feel his eyes on her back as she paced down the corridor, stumbling on the heels that she wasn't quite comfortable with.

As she jabbed the button repeatedly for the elevator to arrive, Rhea tried to balance herself and pull off the stilettos. Suddenly she realized she wasn't alone. She turned around to see Kamal lounging against the wall on the opposite side, looking at her with a heavy-lidded expression which could either mean too much alcohol, or too little sleep. He turned pointedly to look down the passageway, at the door of the cabin she had just rushed out from, which had John standing, hair dishevelled and with his shirt buttons open. The ping of the elevator arriving distracted her from making any comment, and they went in silently. He courteously jabbed the button for her deck and looked her over again, his expression inscrutable.

'Shoes troubling you?'

She nodded in embarrassment, noting dispassionately how perfectly straight his nose was and how his cheekbones could give Benedict Cumberbatch an honourable runners-up mention in a sharp cheekbones contest.

'I don't know what the polite way to say this is, but I think you've got your dress on inside out.'

She gasped in horror, and looked down at herself to find that he was right. The seams were gladly on display for all and sundry to view and comment upon. 'Perhaps,' he continued gently, 'You should check yourself in a mirror next time before stepping out of lover boy's cabin.'

The gall of the man! The absolute gall of him turning up on a deck that wasn't his, and clearly lying in wait for her to emerge from John's cabin. He was a married man, for the love of God! And his wife was on the same cruise, safely deposited in their shared cabin, tucking their kids in bed, while he set off in search of hapless innocents to seduce.

'Why were you following me?' she burst out.

'Following you?' he replied, his voice calm and controlled, almost like he was smothering laughter. 'Why on earth would I do that?'

The elevator slithered to a halt at her deck. 'Mr Kamal Shahani,' she said as the doors opened, holding them open with the button while she gave him a piece of her mind before courage failed her. 'I do know that my aunt asked you to watch out for me in her absence, but this is taking it too far, this is borderline stalking. I don't know what you're trying for but I really am not into married men who are on holiday with their wife and children, and trying to get some action on the side.'

He stared at her with an expression that was shock mingled with disbelief. He began to say something but then decided against it, and clamped his jaw shut so tightly that she could almost see the nerve twitching at the base.

And that was that. As she walked away on trembling legs, hearing the chime of the door shutting behind her, she wondered for a moment why had he not got off on her floor. After all, wasn't that where his cabin was?

FIVE

The next couple of days at sea passed rather uneventfully. Rhea kept to herself or found shaded nooks in areas of the ship where people didn't normally pass through. For most of the time, she stuck to the cabin or the library of the ship where she would be legitimately allowed to stick her nose into a book and not be guilt-tripped into doing something to 'enjoy' herself. To her relief, Rina Maasi was completely into Colonel and seemed okay to leave her niece alone. Plus they were looking forward to Venice.

The excitement of finally visiting Venice had kept Rhea awake all night before the docking and the shore excursion. It was a city she had on her bucket list—the city built on a hundred islands and a warren of narrow canals in which the vaporetti, or water taxis, zipped through in high-speed chases that she had seen in so many movies. The Grand Canal, the Rialto bridge, the brightly-coloured houses with flowers in boxes at the windows, the crumbling palaces, and most of all, the gondolas and the gondoliers. Rhea was reminded of a romance novel cover from her teens—a granite jawed man cuddling a lissome lass on a gondola while the gondolier, his straw-brimmed hat firmly in place, steering forward impassively, his eyes firmly averted from the canoodling couple.

Like on every shore excursion morning, the ship was a rattling tin of repressed excitement, with people rushing through their breakfasts in a bid to quickly get in line for disembarkment. Rina Maasi and Rhea had signed up for the excursion organized by the liner which would pick them up right from the dock at the Venezia Terminali Passeggeri and drop them back in the evening. Rina Maasi had put on her walking shoes and packed strips of knee-pain medicines and joint ache sprays into the little backpack that she always carried on trips like these. Old age made comfort and convenience a virtue over vanity most times.

'Are you sure you are up for it, Rina Maasi?' Rhea asked for the fifth time since morning.

'I'm perfectly fine, but if I keel over and die, fling my body into the Grand Canal and let the fish feed on my corpse,' Maasi said in mock seriousness. 'Come on, darling, it's 8.30 a.m. They'll leave without us and we'll have to swim our way into the city.'

That was Rina Maasi, with a surefire solution to everything that could possibly go wrong and which comprised the most convenient method of disposal of her mortal remains in the event of sudden death.

As they queued up to disembark with all their essentials and documents in hand, they found themselves three people behind a rather familiar, broad pair of shoulders in a linen shirt and khaki cargos. Soon Rhea was unwittingly roped in to play pillar to two pint-sized kids playing hide and seek behind her long legs. She was wearing a pair of knee-length shorts under a blue and white checked cotton shirt, in keeping with the guidelines to have knees and shoulders covered so as to be allowed to enter the Basilica.

It had been a pleasant, if uneventful, time on board with no encounters with married men for the past couple of days. But one glimpse of Kamal's broad shoulders and the butterflies in Rhea's stomach started doing their annoying song and dance act.

'Jay, Kiara,' Naina called, turning around to check the children, and spotted Rina Maasi and Rhea in the queue. 'Oh, hello, good morning! I'm terribly sorry if they've been bothering you. Jay, Kiara . . .' she raised the pitch of her voice in order to bring the little truants to heel. Rhea marvelled at how a slight raise of tone got the kids back into line. Perhaps the answer to world peace was to get mothers to sit in international security council meetings and get opposing nations to shake hands and say sorry through tightly smiling lips.

Kamal turned around and wished them politely. After she had recovered her breath from how perfect he looked, Rhea wondered if he would sparkle in the sunlight. He was, however, looking at her in a manner that was both wary and searching. She hoped Rina Maasi wasn't making a note of that look for further inquisition once they were back on the liner in the evening. He had the caged look of someone who was doing all this against his will, whether it was the polite 'good morning' or the shore excursion, or both.

As they moved forward, Rhea scanned the queue to check if John was in the line. She hadn't seen him since the night she had run off from his cabin like a confused adolescent and was quite unsure as to how he would react if they came face to face. She realized, with a strange sinking feeling, that he hadn't bothered to try to contact her although he knew her cabin. But then, neither had she tried to contact him. They were ships that passed each other in the night, she consoled herself, and smiled at the rather apt metaphor, earning, in turn, an approving smile and a hug from Rina Maasi.

'You should smile more often, Rhea,' she said. 'It lights up your face.'

As they moved along, she spotted John rushing up to the front of the queue and hugging a familiar looking woman, the one he had been dancing with the other night, and handing her a small, compact parcel. His voice floated back to where Rhea stood, a few feet down the line and trying hard to camouflage herself behind a couple of sturdily built Americans. 'Thank you,' she heard him say, the words interspersed among pieces of conversations around. 'Thank you,' he said over and over again. And then he drew the woman close, and kissed her intimately, coupled with some butt-groping that was totally not appropriate in public, especially with children around. Rhea rolled her eyes and looked the other way, all her inner prudishness rising to the fore, until she noticed Kamal looking back at her, his expression as usual, inscrutable.

'Damn! Did he have to be there?' she thought, feeling like an adolescent who had been caught red-handed. But then again, why was she trying to be in his good books? What was it that was making her feel guilty? In fact it was he who should have been guilty of doing what he was, despite being married. She tried hard to think mean thoughts about the delicate Naina who barely came to his shoulder in her canvas soled shoes. Unfortunately, Rhea failed miserably. Naina was a genuinely friendly soul. Pulling herself together, she looked around casually, and noted that Kamal was carrying a bag full of kiddy stuff. Water bottles peeped out from the side pockets and the kids were already mutinying for the chocolates they knew were stashed within. She hoped they were not on the same excursion group—there was only so much of small children tantrums that Rhea could endure for an entire day. Unwittingly, her eyes were drawn to his. Naina was busy chatting with Rina Maasi about boarding schools, how she wanted to put Jay into one, and for her recommendations.

Kamal held a steady gaze that refused to break eye contact despite little hands tugging at the bag, frantic for the cavity inducers. Rhea stared back at him defiantly, until he lowered his gaze to the children clamouring for his attention.

Finally, and after the formalities were completed, they all stepped off the Aqua Princess and emerged blinking into the bright morning light of Venice. Herded in groups, the agenda was a few hours of guided tour through the city, followed by an hour of boat tour of the Grand Canal and other smaller canals. The Basilica, dating back to 1093—as Rhea's well-thumbed guide book told her—was the primary tourist attraction in situ, and not surprisingly, the lines outside were already long.

The plan included a visit to the St Mark's Square and the adjoining prisons, a guided tour into the interior of St Marks Basilica, a walk through the labyrinth of little streets which was the other side of Venice, not visible from the canals. Thereon the tour was to take them to the Campo Santa Maria Formosa, with its Gothic palaces, and Marco Polo's House, a merchant's warehouse, and finally culminating at the fabled Rialto bridge. There was a motorboat launch ride of the Grand Canal scheduled after that as well, something Rina Maasi wasn't too pleased about, wanting instead, a ride on a gondola.

'Venice is a city best self-explored if one has the time,' Kamal told Rina Maasi. They had, through coincidence or devious machinations on Kamal's part, ended up in the same group on the shore excursion. 'You can walk everywhere and where you can't, you take the vaporetto. It is best to just explore the city on your own. I would rather have done that than be herded from place to place. But Naina doesn't trust me to show her the place well.'

'Stick with me, young man,' Rina Maasi commanded imperiously to her ex-student. 'I get a little nervous in a strange city. And I don't want these silly water taxis, I want a gondola ride instead. That is what Venice is all about. Why don't we have a gondola ride?' she asked Rhea, and having confirmed that they did, she continued. 'Why do you want to wander around on your own, Naina? If Kamal knows the city, surely he'll know where to take you around.'

'Hah!' Naina snorted, while trying to restrain her son from attempting back-flips in a crowded piazza. 'Left to Kamal, he'll plead a migraine and will sit at the first table he finds. Or he will get disoriented and end up rambling all over the city and get himself and us lost. Did I tell you what he did the other night after the show that we had all gone to?'

She was not deterred by the lack of invitation to continue her story. 'I sent him off to check on the children and the babysitter and he forgot which deck our cabin was on. He landed on another deck, and almost got taken in by the security for forced entry. Luckily they listened to him about his disorientation and let him go when he showed them the key card to our cabin. He needs to get these migraines checked up. I tell him one day he'll wander off somewhere and get into serious trouble.'

Rhea's heart slammed into her ribcage. *The other night after the show*? That would be when she assumed he had been following her to John's deck. And when she had been rather unpleasant to him. The man had been suffering from disorientation from a debilitating migraine. Rhea wanted to shrink into the shadows and avoid the amused, sardonic gaze of the man they had been discussing and who had been listening to the conversation. At that point Kiara scampered off to investigate a lone pigeon and Naina ran after her.

Kamal shook his head dismissively and turned away. 'She exaggerates,' he said flatly, turning to Rina Maasi. 'It was just a combination of alcohol, a migraine, and sleeplessness. Got off on the wrong deck and wandered around a while before realizing I had emerged on the wrong one. No harm done, except perhaps making some people think of me as a stalker.'

As if on cue, he then expertly lifted Jay onto his shoulders in response to his cries about not being able to see properly. 'Kamal Maama,' Jay called, drawing Kamal's attention to something in the distance, and as he followed the direction of the chubby little finger, Rhea felt her heart plummet to the tips of her candy pink varnished toes.

Maama? Maternal uncle? Which means Naina and Kamal were siblings! Older brother with his younger sister, evidently, and that perhaps explained the rather fraternal vibes the duo gave off which had her perplexed the other day. She darted a curious quick glance to his right hand. There was no ring. The clouds in her brain cleared up and Rhea thanked her stars for not being naked in a bathtub at this eureka moment.

As they moved towards the Basilica, shepherded by Gianni, their allocated guide, who was rattling off the tourist guide version of abbreviated information about the cathedral, warned not to speak once inside, she found herself standing next to Kamal. Jay had been lowered to the ground and was tilting his head up to a scary angle to look at the ceiling, the sheer wonder of something so grand overwhelming his natural rambunctiousness. There was a certain surrealism to the moment—the gold walls reflecting the sunlight coming through the glass windows set high up, the domed ceiling, and the carved wood pews—that remained unaffected by the large number of tourists shuffling their way slowly through the Basilica.

'Errm,' Rhea interjected softly the moment Jay detached himself from his uncle and moved towards the firm grasp of his mother just ahead of them.

'I'm so sorry . . .' she began, thinking back to the heated manner in which she had accused him of stalking her.

Kamal looked at her. 'Did you say something?' She shook her head.

'You did begin to say something and then, perhaps, changed your mind,' he said, his face unsmiling. She noticed, in the light coming through the high glass panes from the domes, that his irises were deep brown with golden reflects that made his eyes look almost feline, yet warm. These were eyes of someone who would be gracious and forgiving of a silly misunderstanding, she told herself. All she had to do was apologize. But why was her heart skipping multiple beats at the sudden realization that, contrary to her belief, he was not a married man?

Rhea squared her shoulders, realizing it would be ungracious not to say what she had begun to. 'Yes, actually I did. I want to apologize for what I said to you the previous night. I assumed you were married to Naina, and never for a moment did I think you were her brother. I mean which brother takes a sister for a cruise with her kids? The normal package is husband, wife, and children, you know.' He looked at her in a deeply disturbing way that set butterflies aflutter again within her digestive organs.

'I cannot imagine what led you to think Naina was my wife. Do we, in any way, give off a married couple vibe? Or was there anything I said to make you think we were? Because that would be really disturbing.'

She frowned. 'No, no, you didn't give off any married vibes to be honest, and you never actually mentioned she was your sister . . . but you don't even look alike! And only married couples travel together with children, so I guess, I just assumed you were married. So where is your spouse?' she stuttered, and then trailed off as she realized the impudence of asking a man she barely knew about his relationship status.

She could have just googled him up, or checked his profile on Facebook. Relationship statuses were there for everyone to see, plus there would have been photographs, appropriately tagged to help her realize that Kamal and Naina were offspring of the same genetic combination. Of course, the gene for height went absconding where Naina was concerned, and the gene for alabaster skin and delicate features passed Kamal by, but those deductions could be drawn later.

Kamal laughed out so loud that a couple of tourists in the immediate vicinity shot them stern and disapproving looks. He shot back an apologetic look and whispered back to her, 'I am neither married, nor divorced, not engaged, and nor seeing anyone. And just to add, I know the same goes for you, so I am not going to ask you that question. As for Naina, she is divorced.'

She looked at him for a long, long moment, feeling all her internal organs lurch around in a drunken manner, bumping against the sternum and the rib cage, and were there lutes playing soft music in the background? As she kept looking, sparkling dust seemed to cloak him and her heart beat so hard that she was sure everyone in a two-kilometre radius could hear it. But no one noticed the vortex of emotions that Rhea had got sucked into. Everything and everyone was normal, carrying on through the tour in a calm manner, completely unaware of the difficulty she had in holding her head and her heart. She held out a hand to steady herself against a banister.

'Are you alright?' Kamal asked.

'I'm fine, I'm fine,' she insisted, leaning back, feeling the ceiling spin around her. He instinctively held out his hand to hold her, gripping her at the waist and drawing her close to him. His eyes bore into hers even as her face flamed a deep red.

Then he suddenly let her go. 'Although nothing would please me more than standing here indefinitely, I need to go take one of them off her hands, or they'll drive her round the bend in ten minutes,' he smiled apologetically. As he broke their physical contact, Rhea quivered at the snap of what felt like a live electrical connection between them.

Snap out of it and stop behaving like a soppy adolescent, she had to tell herself sternly. She looked around for Rina Maasi but couldn't spot the red mop through the teeming crowds. She did a 360 degree turn. No, she was nowhere. A cold, clammy hand of panic gripped her heart.

'Rina Maasi?' she said nervously and in a voice barely audible to herself. She dashed around the cavernous insides. She couldn't spot her anywhere. She grabbed Gianni, their tour guide, by the arm and whispered urgently, 'Have you seen my aunt anywhere?'

'She was right here . . .' he said, and was surprised when he realized that the elderly lady was nowhere in the vicinity.

Kamal sauntered back with Jay perched once again on his shoulders. 'I can't see Rina Maasi around, can you?' Rhea was panicking now. Her heart was thudding erratically, her palms clammy with sweat.

Kamal looked around. 'No I can't,' he said matter-of-factly. He went and peered into the various possible corners that an elderly lady might find a spot to sit and rest an aching leg, but came back shaking his head in the negative.

'She is not here. And she's quite easily noticeable from a distance.'

Yup, with her red hair and the hot pink blouse she had on, Rina Maasi was hard to miss. Rhea started pacing around.

'Perhaps she stepped out to get some fresh air? Kamal said.

That seemed like a possibility. He rounded up Naina, explaining the missing-aunt situation, grabbed Kiara by hand, lowered Jay back on ground, and moved them all towards the exit.

Naina patted Rhea's back and tried to calm her down. Her eyes were gentle and understanding—what was it about this girl, who was almost her age, that made her seem so much older, wiser, and heartbroken, Rhea wondered. 'Don't worry, she will be found, she couldn't have gone far. She'll probably be out somewhere, waiting for us to emerge.'

All the worst-case scenarios ran amok on the wide screen of Rhea's imagination—Rina Maasi having a heart failure and collapsing in a corner within the Basilica, her cold corpse found by cleaners in the morning, or her being dragged off at knifepoint by hoodlums who make her take off her jewellery and hand it over before slitting her throat. Rhea gulped in horror at the prospects her imagination threw at her. Looking around with fast escalating concern, they emerged into the bright sunlight of the Venetian morning. The tourists thronged the Piazza and there were pigeons fluttering everywhere. But Rina Maasi was nowhere to be seen.

Then it struck her. 'She's probably gone off to hunt for some souvenirs—Murano glassware, ceramics and such. Are there any stores nearby? She is not one for too much history and prefers to get straight to where the shopping is,' Rhea said.

Kamal turned to Gianni. 'What should we do? Can we put out an alert for her, file a police complaint?'

Gianni was reassuring, yet confused. 'Geev me one mineet please,' he said, pulling out his mobile phone and proceeding to have rapid fire conversations in Italian which she could not understand but Kamal seemed to, judging by his eyes firmly fixed on Gianni as he spoke.

'Why don't you and Naina sit here, with the children, while Gianni and I scan the square for Soni Ma'am. Now that I think of it, I last saw her walking with that elderly gentleman from Chandigarh. He seems to have disappeared from sight as well.'

'What do we do, what do we do?' Rhea moaned, 'Where could she disappear? I hope she's all right and nothing has happened to her. She didn't even carry her phone along this morning, insisting she wouldn't need it.'

Naina sat down firmly on one of the conveniently placed benches, handed out liquid refreshments to her offspring, and gestured that Rhea should sit down too. 'There's no point panicking, or all of us running around like headless chickens searching for her. I suggest you sit here like Kamal said and let them look around. Perhaps she has just wandered off and hasn't realized that she has got separated from the group. She couldn't have gone far.'

Rhea acknowledged the wisdom of the statement and felt the need for a caffeine shot to soothe her frayed nerves. It was bad enough that her aunt had gone missing, she was also cursed to go berserk over all the mental calculations of converting Euro to rupee before even considering to buy herself a cup of coffee and not feel guilty. Everything was so expensive!

A few minutes later, she saw Kamal leading a grim looking Rina Maasi, followed by Colonel Singh, towards them. Gianni followed, his face split into two by a grin so wide that it seemed the corners of his mouth were held together by rubber bands.

'Look who we found around the corner, shopping frantically for souvenirs!' Kamal laughed.

'You gave me such a scare Rina Maasi!' Rhea squealed, rushing up to hug her and feeling silly about the two tears that inadvertently escaped her eyes. She was not given to such wanton displays of emotion and looked up guiltily to see Kamal's eyes on her. The expression in them was surprisingly tender.

'Soni Ma'am and Colonel Singh, I must insist you stick to the group now, or if you go missing again we will leave for the ship without you,' Kamal said wryly, his voice serious, but his eyes laughing.

'Young lad,' Rina Maasi said sharply, 'We are of a certain age when we need to find restrooms at regular intervals. We were merely trying to locate some facilities and had to walk quite a lot to find one.'

'You aska me next time you wanta go to restroom, madam,' Gianni interjected helpfully, his hands gesturing animatedly that there were public toilets everywhere his hand pointed, if only she had cared to ask him.

'If you pull this disappearing act on me once again I will make you wear an adult diaper for the next shore excursion,' Rhea hissed into her aunt's ear as a mock warning, relief washing over finally. But Rina Maasi, indefatigable as always, hissed right back, 'If you do, I will make you change the soiled one.'

Harmony restored, they got on with their scheduled sightseeing. As they moved out of the square, to visit Doge's palace, Rhea noticed the same middle-aged woman John had handed the parcel to on board the Aqua Princess, chatting with someone who looked like a local. She pulled out the same parcel from her handbag, handed it to the man and walked off. Strange, Rhea thought, that John should be on ship and not come on shore to hand over the parcel in person. But then there was a lot about John that she didn't understand. Point to ponder upon later, she told herself. Right now she had to thank the forces above that Rina Maasi was found, safe and sound, and also that Kamal Shahani was not married.

The rest of the afternoon, which was rather hot, was spent walking around the streets of the city, eating more gelato than was mandated, picking up souvenirs for friends and family back home, clicking pictures, and doing other usual touristy stuff, followed by a motor boat ride through the canals. Rina Maasi wanted to shop some more but they had just enough time to scramble back to the ship with the final horn.

'I'm exhausted!' Maasi said as soon as she hit the bed. The cabin had been restored to its pristine self in their absence, complete with chocolates on the pillows for the sugar rush that was needed after a long day of traipsing around on foot. 'I'm just going to lie down and will order in dinner if I feel hungry. But I don't think I will. Isn't he so handsome?'

Rhea swivelled around, perplexed at where the conversation was headed. 'Yes, he so is,' she replied, her face colouring up at the memory of his arm around her waist and the touch searing her skin into flames.

'Such a gentleman,' Rina Maasi continued.

'Yes, he is,' Rhea agreed, realizing that she hadn't met many of his kind in recent times. Perhaps their population was diminishing.

'And he still has all his hair . . .' Rina Maasi sighed. 'By the time most men reach Bikram's age, they either have a toupee or a comb over like a horrible giant spider squatting on an egg.' Rhea laughed despite herself. They were talking about two different men. As if on cue, there was a sharp rap at the door just then, and the man whose head was still full of hair entered.

'Rina, my dear,' the Colonel's voice boomed. 'Care for a quiet meal in the cabin, rather than the noisy restaurant tonight? My legs have quite given up on me with all that walking.' The ex-army man had had his left leg blown off in combat. The prosthesis was rather unforgiving and after long use it chaffed against the stump and caused soreness. He was limping discernibly and sank into a chair with a sigh. 'The kids want to go watch a movie, and my son and his wife are going to the bar and then dancing.'

'Of course, Bikramjit,' Rina Maasi cooed, 'I was thinking of dining in anyway. I have no stamina to walk another step.'

Rhea decided it was appropriate to make herself scarce, and announced bravely that she was going to meet friends for dinner at the Indian restaurant on board.

She showered quickly, changed into a comfortable cotton sheath dress in baby pink and ate a solitary meal at the restaurant she claimed she had to meet friends at. She finished her meal and wondered whether she should get back to the cabin or wander around a bit and find herself a party to join. It was then she spotted him, standing at the end of the deck below, looking out at the blackness of the ocean. She rushed down, scattering unwary people in her wake. By the time she reached where he was, Rhea was panting heavily.

Kamal was freshly showered—his hair was still damp—and was clad in a jacket over a pair of trousers. His hands clasped the railing and his shoulders were hunched forward, leaning over it. She went and stood next to him without speaking a word, looking out at the sea fluttering under them. The waves rippled delicately as the great liner cut through the sea, reflecting the lights of the ship, and it was as if a ghost ship and ghost figurines living right below, in the ocean, were keeping them company through their journey.

The sun had long set over the horizon and the coast was twinkling at a distance. The first stars of the evening sky made their sparkling entrance, the solemn moon rose from behind a cloud and lit up their faces.

'Hello,' she said quietly, wondering if she was intruding upon him.

He turned to look at her, his eyes smiled.

'So, Rhea Khanna, is that why you have been so prickly with me? Did you put me down as a lecherous, philandering husband? And that I was hitting on you despite being a married man, on cruise with his family?'

She nodded, embarrassed and speechless. 'How could you? She's my kid sister. I've brought her on this cruise to cheer her up. She's just been through hell—an ugly divorce and a custody battle.'

'How was I to know?' Rhea defended herself hotly. 'Brothers and sisters are supposed to look similar.'

He threw his head back and laughed aloud, a deep rolling laugh that was full throated and unhindered.

'You are such a naïve one. Perhaps we could be step-brother and sister. Perhaps we could just resemble parents who don't look similar . . .' his voice trailed off as he leaned back to stare at her. Her knees turned into jelly and threatened to buckle under her. 'I cannot believe you thought I was a sleaze ball hitting on you when the wife's back was turned, and with my children right there. And here I was, wondering what had I done to upset you so.' He laughed again.

She drew away from him. 'Do you blame me? You didn't introduce Naina as your sister!'

'My apologies,' he replied. 'Can you forgive me, can I make you forgive me?' he added in mock seriousness, before bending down to explore her lips. She put her arms around him, drinking in the freshly bathed muskiness of him, her fingers tugging at his damp hair, feeling his hands grip her waist urgently, pulling her harder against his body. She let her hands travel all over the muscled planes of his body, slipping them through the thin linen shirt he had on, under his jacket. As they broke away to look at each in wonder, she gently pushed him away, albeit reluctantly.

'No, no, I just wanted to apologize for being rude to you,' she said. His hands refused to relinquish the grip on her waist. He gently tucked an errant lock of hair back behind her ear and began nibbling her ear in a manner that made her forget all the moral lessons she had learnt on her mother's knee.

'Stop,' she said, fighting herself more than him, and pushed him away. 'We must stop. I'm not looking for a holiday fling.' He pulled himself away and looked at her. Just then, thick drops of rain began slapping down on them from a sudden cloud that found itself over the ship. All over the deck, people began to scuttle for cover.

'Why do you think that I want a holiday fling?'

Rhea did not wait to listen to him. She pulled herself away and ran swiftly into the covered parts of the deck, and from there to the elevators that would take her back to her cabin. She opened the door to find Rina Maasi asleep and snoring gently, which was a blessing because she spent the rest of the night tossing his last sentence over and over again in her mind. What did he want from her if not a holiday fling?

SIX

By the time sleep embraced her, the first rays of the morning sun had spread across the sky. The weather had cleared after a brief shower and Rhea could hear the routine morning sounds—Rina Maasi waking up, brushing her teeth, gargling her throat long and laboriously, switching on the kettle, possibly sipping her cup of tea whilst sitting by the window, surveying all that was spread before her.

A gentle breeze from the open window stirred the room and played on Rhea's skin, making it impossible for her to bask in further laziness. She stretched on the bed languorously when memory of the previous night's kiss came right back to her. She sat up with a start.

He had kissed her last night, a deep, long drawn out kiss and she had kissed him right back. Had she not broken away where would it have ended? Though her imagination ran wild, the sane, rational part of her brain told her calmly that there probably wasn't much they could have done on the open deck for fear of being arrested for public indecency.

Why had she never felt like this when Samir had kissed her? Why had it always been an exercise in hurrying through the kissing in order to get to the act in question with him? Just one kiss with Kamal made Rhea realize that perhaps, after all these years, she had never really been kissed the way she was meant to be kissed.

She rushed to the bathroom and splashed water on her face, hoping to douse the sudden, flaming red that had stained her cheeks. When she came out, with thoughts suitably collected and composed, Rina Maasi was pouring herself what seemed like a second cup of tea.

'Join me?' she asked. Rhea poured herself a cup and sat down on the chair opposite.

Her aunt's wise eyes settled on her with a twinkling, discerning look. 'Now, young lady,' she said, 'Is there something you should be telling me, or do I come to all sorts of conclusions by myself?'

'About what, Rina Maasi?' Rhea asked. She had always been scrupulously honest about her relationships and love life with her aunt.

'About why you were giving sheepish glances at my ex-student all of yesterday.'

Rhea blushed prettily and looked away.

Rina Maasi narrowed her eyes and looked intently at her. 'Don't tell me you are falling for the boy?' There was a gentleness in her voice that belied the sternness of her glance.

Rhea laughed. 'Come on, Rina Maasi, I am a responsible adult. You don't have to babysit me.'

'I know, I know, but here, on this cruise, you are under my supervision and I can't have you getting your heart broken again. Not when you're finally managing to smile and look human again instead of Frankenstein's monster's bride with an intestinal tract that needs more roughage.'

'Seriously, Maasi, no danger of heartbreak here, trust me.'

'You asked me to trust you when you announced your engagement with that sphincter-clenched specimen, and I did. I don't trust you anymore. Did you sleep with him last night?' Trust Rina Maasi to do away with gentle delicacy on such matters.

'No!' Rhea squawked, appalled at her aunt's unabashed lowering of her moral compass. 'I barely know him. Anyway, what's with the Spanish Inquisition level questions, Maasi?'

Rina Maasi raised a single eyebrow, in a manner perfected in extricating confessions from young striplings about pranks such as Fevikwick applied to chairs, necessitating holes being cut in the seat of a hapless Maths teacher's trousers.

'I hope you know that this cruise is barely for a few weeks. Then you get back to India, to different cities, and get on with your respective lives. And what do you know about him anyway?'

Rhea looked out of the porthole, noting the never changing sameness of the sea. As the sun rose higher in the firmament, the waters reflected its rays off its surface and the sky changed its hues quietly, from a soft pink to a beautiful golden. This was not a discussion she preferred to have on an empty stomach.

For a moment there was an awkward silence between aunt and niece while each weighed their words, reluctant to say something that might rub the other the wrong way.

'Don't get me wrong, child. I don't want you to get hurt again. I brought you on this cruise with me to get your mind off Samir. I want you to heal, Rhea. I don't want you to let your vulnerability make you rush into something on the rebound, a casual fling that both of us know won't last once you land back in India. You have always been an emotional, sensitive child and you get easily hurt.'

Rina Maasi was making sense, Rhea acknowledged sadly. 'Yes, Maasi, you are right. I do find myself terribly attracted to him although for the longest time ever I was terribly rude to him because I thought he was hitting on me despite being married. It was only yesterday that I realized Naina was his sister.'

A hearty chuckle emerged from Rina Maasi. 'That's funny, I thought the same until he introduced Jay to me as his nephew on the second day of our trip, when he came to check up on me.'

Rhea gasped. She had been the only person labouring under the misconception that Kamal was married with offspring!

'No damage done yet, Rhea,' Rina Maasi said with the warmth of someone who knew what it was to be confused about love. 'But don't go head over heels at the deep end. You were always an intense child, you made best friends too soon, you fought with them too quickly . . .'

'No worries of getting emotionally involved with him, Rina Maasi,' she said, feeling her heart break into the proverbial thousand pieces as she spoke, and realizing that she needed to tell herself that. Technically Kamal and she hadn't even been on a date, unless traipsing around an Italian city in a herd of strangers could be called a date.

The cabin phone rang. 'Who could it be so early in the morning?' Rina Maasi wondered aloud. Rhea set her cup down and padded over to the phone at the side of the bed in her bare feet. 'Hello?' she asked hesitantly.

'You left without completing our conversation,' said the voice at the other end of the line, still husky with sleep. 'Was I so terrible a kisser?'

'It wasn't the kiss,' she whispered as softly as she could, aware that Rina Maasi was listening intently, and she had no need of hearing aids yet. 'It was me. I'm not in a place right now where I can handle a relationship, or even a holiday fling.'

'That is exactly what we need to discuss, Rhea,' he said, 'I need to meet you.'

'No,' she replied, her tone definite and regretful. 'There is nothing to discuss, no need to meet. Let's forget that kiss happened. Good bye, Kamal.' With that, she put the phone down.

Rina Maasi looked at her curiously as she moved back towards the chairs by the window.

'That was Kamal,' she told her. 'I told him that we couldn't let this go further.'

'It's for the best, my child,' Rina Maasi said, reaching out a perfectly manicured, wrinkled hand, and patting her head with it. 'When you get back home, you will realize how right I was. You don't want to try and heal one wound by digging another next to it.'

Rina Maasi knew a thing or two about broken relationships. Her own marriage was a fly by night thing and she was divorced before the mehndi faded from her palms. She never married again and lived her life alone despite being the looker among the three sisters.

'Yes, Rina Maasi,' she replied mechanically, feeling her voice go flat and the light dim in her eyes.

'Anyway, enough of discussing men, what do you plan to do today?' Maasi asked. 'I'm a little exhausted. I think all this gallivanting around on shore excursions is not a great option, especially when your heart almost stops on you some nights ago. I'm going to stay put in the cabin . . . perhaps catch up on some reading. But you go out and wander the ship.'

Rhea raised one eyebrow at her aunt, knowing there had to be more to it than a genuine desire to have her wander the ship on her own. 'Are you sure Rina Maasi?' she asked. 'Won't you get bored on your own?'

'Oh no, didn't I mention? Bikramjit will be joining me soon and we are going to play cards till lunch time. After that we will go for a ballroom dancing lesson.'

Rhea laughed. Her aunt may have just delivered a long sermon on not getting involved in a holiday romance, yet she was headed the same path with the Colonel. 'Sure, Rina Maasi. I will take myself out and you can have all the calmness and quietude that you need to restore your spirits.'

Rina Maasi rolled her eyes. 'I think I will skip breakfast. My digestive power isn't what it used to be and I think I over indulged at dinner last night.'

'Now, please, don't discuss your digestive system with the Colonel.' Rhea winced at the thought of it.

'Why not, my dear? At our age, it is the most interesting topic we have to discuss.'

Rhea bathed quickly, put on a pair of floral shorts with a cropped white vest that left just a bit of her waist visible for public viewing over one of the more daring purchases she had made for her intended honeymoon, a white and gold bikini. She dunked a floppy straw hat on her head to keep the sun off her face, pulled a pair of floral printed, woven, straw-soled espadrilles, and completed her look with a pair of huge Jackie O sunglasses that almost covered her entire face, before emerging blinking into the bright morning sunlight on the deck.

As she set off to check the activities offered on board, she zeroed in on the rock climbing wall to begin with, followed by a dip in the pool and a day spent lazing along the poolside. But when she reached the wall she realized that despite the encouraging instructors, she didn't have the courage to try it on her own.

'You have just one life; be reckless,' she told herself in a vain bid to boost up her non-existent courage. For a girl whose zenith of risk-taking was limited to crossing the road when the traffic had not yet halted, even in a traffic jam, a rock climbing wall was Everest. Perhaps she could take a dance lesson on doing the tango—the ship's newsletter had announced it would be held at around this time in one of the dance halls. It was high time she exchanged one of her two left feet for a right one. Samir was a wonderful dancer and she had always been embarrassed to be with him on the dance floor where they were obviously mismatched. Had they been mismatched in other areas as well? He was unpredictable, unlike her, and that's what made their journey such a fun ride. Damn him. He still kept sneaking into her thoughts even though she tried hard to keep him out. She closed her eyes tight.

Damn it all, she was going to spend the day doing absolutely nothing except get tanned by the poolside, watch the movies they showed on the big screen, and allow herself to pig out on the snacks and sandwiches from the 24 hour café. After all, a broken heart hurriedly scotch-taped together into functionality, not to mention the bruised ego, needed meaningless calories to heal well.

There were two pools—one mid-ship where the maximum action was, plus the screen for movie watching, and the other on the top deck which was meant only for adults and was more secluded, but had a fabulous view of the open sea from every point. She opted for the mid-ship pool, thinking she could catch a movie if she felt like it. And it would be nice to be in the thick of things—the children's paddle pools by the side, the hot tubs, the choice between deck chairs and chaise lounges.

The poolside, as it was on most days at sea, was packed to the gills. Every sun bed was covered with bodies in varying stages of undress, painstakingly rubbing tanning lotion on each other in a vain bid to get the golden glow they craved. Some of those sprawled on the deckchairs had skin which had already crossed the Rubicon dividing it from a golden glow to fiery, burnt leather. Rhea spotted a couple of empty chaise lounges in the covered area and pounced on one swiftly before it was snapped up by another poolside prowler.

'Mummeeee, Mummeee,' the insistent squeals for attention hit her eardrums, 'Jay is pushing me.'

She lifted her head from the book that she had just opened and saw Naina approaching, accompanied by Jay and Kiara who were busy swatting each other in Punch and Judy manner. Naina waved happily as she spotted her.

'Hey Rhea, good to see you, just hold this for a moment,' she said, unloading what seemed to be a plethora of arm floats onto Rhea's deck chair before getting down to help her children out of their clothes. They had their swim suits on underneath and their mother then put their arm floats on with practiced ease.

'Thanks,' she said, 'I'll just put them in the kiddy pool under the lifeguard's watch and be right back. Don't let anyone take the other chair.' Putting her bag and things on the chair to indicate it was booked, she sauntered off, holding a child with each hand.

True to her word, she was back a couple of minutes later and shrugged off her flowing, floral sarong to flaunt a teeny-weeny bikini that revealed more than it concealed. Rhea felt positively overdressed in comparison in her more modest white bikini which was held together by large gold rings and which had her cousin, who had gone shopping with her, dare her to try it on.

'Didn't see you at dinner last night,' Naina said settling down after adjusting her deck chair to ensure she was completely in the shade and rubbing big dollops of sunblock on her exposed skin.

'Oh, Rina Maasi was too tired, so she ate in the cabin and I grabbed a bite at the Indian restaurant on level three,' she answered. 'I think I've reached my threshold of eating Continental, Italian and World Cuisine and now want my rajma chawal.'

'Me too, me too,' Naina chortled. 'I cannot tell you how much I am missing my cook from back home. I wish I could have flown him out with us. The kids are being so fussy about food, it's driving me up the wall.'

A waiter came by with the drinks they had ordered—two tall glasses of Long Island Iced Tea, and Naina sipped on hers delicately. A group of Americans, loud and blotchy from the sun, were playing a rambunctious game of improvised water polo and loud cheers were going up from the deckchairs fringing the pool whenever points were scored. Some of the ship's officers had joined in too, she noticed.

'It has been draining, this heat. Who would have thought it would be so hot here? It's almost like being back in Mumbai in May.'

'Or Delhi in May. No, not quite Delhi in May,' Rhea said, fishing out her sunblock and rubbing her legs down.

'I'm so glad though that I came on this trip,' Naina continued, almost as if she was glad to find adult company to speak in full sentences and not have to punctuate those sentences with 'No, Don't Do That', at periodic intervals. 'I didn't want to.'

'Why is that?' Rhea asked, squinting against the bright morning sun that was lighting up the deck in a blaze of golden light that made sunglasses mandatory to protect the eyes. Rhea often hid behind huge dark sunglasses, it made avoiding eye contact possible and offered her a sense of being hidden even in a crowd.

'My divorce just came through and I was rather depressed. You can imagine, no husband and two children to bring up . . . the man is being a scrooge about the alimony and child support, so it feels a little scary. But my parents and Kamal have been tremendously supportive. Kamal especially won't let me wallow in misery, so he booked us on this cruise and wouldn't take no for an answer. He's always been such a bossy, big brother.' Naina smiled, her expression softening. 'Now I need to get back on my feet and decide on how best to use that business management degree that I have.'

Rhea nodded absent-mindedly, thinking back to the kiss she shared with the bossy, big brother mentioned, the previous night. She had to chide herself for being silly and come back to the present. 'Of course, Kamal is convincing me to join him in his company. He could do with the help, he says, but I know what he's really trying to do—he wants to make it easy for me. Give me a job so I don't feel like I am a burden on him.'

She paused, lost in thought. 'I'll see what I can do, but I think it's time to think about him now. He needs to settle down,' she announced melodramatically after the brief pause, like she had figured out the answer to life. Settle down . . . didn't she know only tea leaves 'settled down', Rhea thought mean-spiritedly.

'My mother wants grandchildren. From her son, of course, this time. Now only if he would settle down with a good girl, my parents would be so relieved. He just broke up with a girl and has finally agreed to let my parents call the professional matchmakers in. But it's so difficult to find a girl who fits in with all the parameters he has listed—good looking, from a cultured family, well educated . . .' she sighed. 'My mother's greatest fear is that if we don't find someone suitable for him some mercenary gold digger will get her claws into him.'

Rhea listened without comment, thankful she had the sunglasses on to mask her expression. A churning had begun in her insides that the Long Island Ice Tea was doing nothing to quell.

She wished they could change the topic to something less incendiary to her gastric juices, and promptly asked Naina about the sarong she wore. It was available in the swimwear store at the shopping boulevard, she was informed, and she had picked it up along with the swimsuit she was wearing.

'How insensitive of me. You have just emerged from a broken engagement,' she said in an apologetic tone. 'Your aunt told me about it yesterday, and all I am talking about is getting my brother engaged.'

'Don't be silly,' Rhea replied, deciding to play back in the same vein. 'You've just got a divorce too. We are all moving on from our wounds.'

'And we refuse to build monuments of our hurt,' Naina said, draining her glass and setting it down grimly. 'Now when Kamal gets married and has children, my parents will do their *chardham yatra* of the modern age—my mom has announced she's going to go on a year-long cruise around the world.'

'That sounds wonderful,' Rhea said, envious of the idea of navigating the world in luxury, like a modern-day explorer, for a year.

'But before that he is still to agree to meet with any of the girls my parents have shortlisted . . .' she stopped short. 'Hey Kamal, come join us!' she called out. A shadow announced itself over Rhea who was lying with her back to the sun, enjoying the feel of the warm rays on her skin.

'Let me not intrude into your conversation. I'm just looking for a spot to sit and check my mails,' he said grabbing a chair and went into the little alcove which offered a plug and Wi-Fi. Quickly immersing himself in his laptop, he began tapping on the keyboard furiously, a slight frown of concentration appearing on his forehead and dividing his brow, and spoke into his phone in a subdued tone. Rhea took a quick glance at him from behind the safety of her sunglasses. He was stubble jawed and distracted, and scowled into the distance while speaking on the phone.

'Let me go check on the kids and see if they want to come out,' Naina said and before Rhea could protest about being left alone, she rose gracefully and walked off towards the pool. For lack of anything to do and the awareness of a piercing gaze on her at regular intervals, Rhea pulled out her SPF 60 dry touch sunblock and began applying it on her arms which were beginning to sting with the sun's rays. She was in a lazy, languid mood, and the sun and sea breeze made her sleepy. She squeezed out some lotion and tried to apply it on her back unsuccessfully when the tube was plucked out of her hand and strong hands began to stroke the sunblock lotion on her. Without turning her head, Rhea knew who it was. Kamal. He sat beside her on the chaise lounge and her body tingled from the touch of his fingers on her bare skin.

None of them said a word. Kamal worked his hands over her neck and shoulders, down her back and up her arms. Smooth, rhythmic strokes. He pushed her gently down onto her stomach, his fingers deftly unclasping her bikini top, leaving her entire back bare to his touch. His palms moved together in perfect synchronization. Each movement, each touch made her body dissolve into nothingness. His hands were warm and smooth, and moved on her skin with confidence, waking up every nerve ending that came in contact and set them on fire. A part of her realized she should protest, should ask him to stop—this was dangerously intimate—but she couldn't. Rhea's senses became alive as she felt the heat of his body barely millimetres away, the length of his thigh along her back, his muscles hard and tense, and his hands on her skin, slow and sensuous.

'Don't . . .' she began, weakly, her resolve melting under the touch of his hands. 'Shhh . . .' he whispered back is his throaty voice. 'Don't say a thing, just relax.' He stroked the length of her back with both hands, pressing his palm flat against her skin, kneading her shoulders gently at first, and then more insistently, so she gasped with pleasure.

'Your muscles are too tense,' he muttered. 'You need to relax.' She felt her body melt into longing, her toes curling with pleasure, and moans of delight escaping her inadvertently. She desperately wanted to turn her body towards him and draw him close, to kiss him deep and feel his skin, bare and warm, against hers, to put his head to her bare breasts and feel his hungry lips on them. And then, just as suddenly as he had begun, he stopped. It felt like an electric current had been switched off. She moaned in protest for him to continue.

He gently refastened her bikini clasp. 'I don't normally go around giving back rubs to girls I'm supposed to watch out for. But you make me break all my rules.'

She buried her face into the towel she had spread out on the deck chair and tried to calm herself down before turning around to face him. If she did, she knew, she would reveal the yearning that had suffused her body. But by the time Rhea dared to lift her head and look around, he was gone from sight, swallowed into the elevators that led down to the cabins.

SEVEN

For Rhea, the next couple of days at sea were spent basking by the poolside in hope, unacknowledged to herself, that Kamal would pass by and more sunscreen would be applied. She even carried along an extra-large tube of the SPF 60, always prepared, like a good girl scout. But she slipped terribly in her own commitment to sunscreen application, as a result of which by day three she was tanned to nutmeg levels.

'Oh my God, what have you done to yourself!' Rina Maasi gasped as Rhea entered the cabin.

'You've ruined your complexion.' Rina Maasi was of the school of thought that believed a woman's complexion was her prized possession, and exposing it to the elements lowered her attractiveness quotient. All the backlash to fairness cream campaigns had completely passed her by.

'Haven't I told you to always carry an umbrella? And wear a cap? And put on sunblock? Look at yourself!'

'Come on Rina Maasi, it's just a tan, it will wear off. A tan is exotic, it is proof one has been on holiday. I need proof I had been away,' Rhea replied, noting that two plates of lunch were yet to be cleared and there seemed to have been rather hectic bridge playing with the cards kept untidily on the side table.

'It causes skin cancer,' Rina Maasi said darkly, all doom and gloom, casting an eagle eye over Rhea's exposed skin for immediate evidence of fledgling melanomas. 'And you have proof. Those selfies with cheeks sucked in so you look like a skeleton against every monument we've visited.'

'A tan is exotic,' Rhea argued. 'A tan acquired on the Mediterranean even more!'

'Darling child, we live in a country where you can get a tan by putting your nose outside a window, a tan means nothing for us tropical climate folks. This is just skin damage. It will age you before your time.'

'Anyway,' Rhea cut in, 'We need to get dressed and be ready by 7.30 p.m. It's formal dining tonight. The Captain's Gala Dinner, in case you had forgotten,' she reminded her aunt.

'I haven't, and by the way, your mother called to tell me how you were always too busy to call her back whenever she has messaged. Call her sometime today, will you?'

'I will, I'm sorry.' Feeling contrite for ignoring them because she didn't feel like talking, Rhea truly adored her parents. It was difficult, though, to be in a conversation with her mother for over five minutes and not get into an argument over the emotional guilt trip that she insisted on taking her daughter on. And as for her father, retired principal of a reputed school, having taught some of the brightest and best in the country, his shame was that his only surviving offspring made nothing of herself worth mentioning in public. She had barely redeemed herself by getting engaged to a 'good' boy working in a multinational company in a senior position, then the engagement broke up. Rhea could do no good in her father's eyes. They were perennial antagonists and her long suffering mother often played referee between the two.

Rina Maasi yawned long and wide enough for all her well-tended teeth to be visible. 'There's so much walking on these ships, first from here to the elevator bank, then from the atrium to the formal dining room, by the end of it my varicose veins protest vociferously. You know, my knees aren't what they used to be. Perhaps I should sit this one out.' She paused and stretched, rising up from her chair and wandering towards the wardrobe. Her determined expression faltered.

'This is too tempting, though. A formal night, and Navin told me he had pulled strings to get us seated at the table next to the Captain's.' Navin was the ex-student who now headed operations at the travel agency that gave Rina Maasi a fabulous discount for two for this cruise. Rina Maasi opened the wardrobe and began riffling determinedly through the clothes she had brought along. 'Perhaps a sari,' she said, holding a soft beige chiffon with silver threads against herself. Rhea approved whole-heartedly. It was a sea change from the hot pinks and reds she had been blotting the landscape with over the past few days.

Rhea had nothing in the formal line of wear, except for a long, slinky, beaded, black and gold gown with a low cowl back which did not allow any inner wear but strategic application of double sided tape and a thong. It was a little risqué and not something she would have picked for herself but, come on, she had been shopping for her honeymoon! She also had the perfect black and gold stilettos to go with it, with thin delicate straps and gold beads stitched on them.

She pulled it off the hanger and laid it on the bed before getting into the shower. There wasn't much to scrub off—sunbathing in the middle of the sea allowed only so much grime to settle—and she was done in a jiffy. When she emerged, Rina Maasi was already draped in the sari, having paired it with a muted brocade blouse and a choker of amber stones snug against her neck. The effect of the chic ensemble was however ruined by heavy application of face paint. Rhea took a tissue and toned it down, steadfastly ignoring her aunt's protests.

When she had been a young girl, Rhea would stare with open-mouthed fascination as Rina Maasi got dressed-up for her parties and functions and learnt at her knee how to apply eyeliner and blend eye shadow. Now that she had grown up, the roles were reversed. 'You look really lovely, Maasi,' Rhea said. 'Don't mind me saying so, but you have absolutely lovely skin for your age, and you can carry off soft colours so well, both in clothes and make-up. Most people can't. Perhaps you should experiment with a lighter palette. I could get you an appointment with an image consultant to understand more, you know, on which colours to choose, including . . .' she winced, '. . . for your hair.' Rina Maasi looked at herself after half the make-up she had applied had been plied off. 'I would like that, yes. I could do with some make-up lessons. Basically what you're trying to tell me, child, is that less is more, and I get it now.'

Maasi may have aged but she had not mellowed. So despite the soft wrinkles that made their way across her skin, this fieriness added to her attractiveness. Rhea wished she had inherited some of her aunt's zeal. She was instead a diluted, parental guidance version of Maasi's sharp featured beauty.

Rina Maasi beamed happily. 'Thank you, my darling. Now let me see you in that rather daring dress that you've laid out. I can guarantee some eyes will be out on stalks this evening and some necks might get sprained in order to catch a glimpse of that back as you pass by. I hope you have no intention of revealing more than one cleavage this evening?'

'Come on Maasi, I barely have one cleavage to begin with. And this is positively staid compared to what some of the women will be wearing.'

'Well,' Rina Maasi harrumphed, 'I hope you've brought along enough double sided tape because you're going to need it with that. Where are my seasickness pills . . .' Her voice trailed off as she began rummaging through the little pile on the table by her bed.

Rhea changed into the dress and looked at herself critically in the mirror. Luckily, the formal dining room would be softly lit with golden lighting, as she had noted from her previous experiences there, meaning that she could afford to skip the base. The sun had kissed her skin tone into a deeper, mysterious hue. A quick dab of bronzer to highlight her cheeks and eyes, a dark line over her upper eyelids and on the inside of her lower lid, a lashing of mascara, topped by a soft application of a neutral shimmery gloss over her lips and she was ready to go. She kept her hair style simple—just washed and finger dried into waves which she pinned back behind one ear, letting the waves cascade down on one shoulder and leaving her back clear. If she closed her eyes, Rhea could still feel Kamal's fingers on her bare back. Turning her thoughts back to the present, she put on her heels and when she finally emerged, all dressed up, Rina Maasi let out a wolf whistle so salacious that Rhea could swear she learnt it from a sailor.

'Ready, are we?' she asked, holding out her hand and having Rhea help her to her feet. 'Let's go get them, tiger.'

Rhea rolled her eyes and laughed. Rina Maasi was incorrigible.

As they made their way to the dining hall, they met other faces, now familiar, and smiled politely, exchanged pleasantries. Rhea was once again struck by the lack of single people on the cruise. The entire passenger list seemed to be divided evenly between retired people and families and honeymooning couples. Already seated at their allotted table were the Colonel, his son and daughter-in-law.

The Captain's Gala Dinner was perhaps the most formal night on board the ship. On this occasion, not only would guests on the ship get the opportunity to actually be able to don their shiniest best formals, but also tuck down a meal of iconic levels that would have them sated and spent with gastronomic afterglow. There wasn't dancing. But there was champagne and the chance to hobnob with the captain and the other main officers of the ship, and get photographed with them.

As they were steered to their table, Rhea noticed Kamal and Naina being directed towards the same direction. Her heart lurched unbecomingly. Damn him, he had absolutely no business looking like a young Brando, with the same half smile, and the-world-is-my-oyster gaze.

As he came up to the table and bent down to greet and hug Maasi, she looked at him discreetly, under her mascaraed lashes. It was endearing, the way he was so gentle and polite with Rina Maasi, she thought. But why did he have to look so delectable? Men like him who were a feast to the eyes should not be allowed to wear dinner jackets and cause an increase in heart rates all around, she thought, gasping for air. Just as she tried to look away, their eyes met for a brief moment, and despite herself, she was drawn back to looking into them. She could feel her breathing going ragged and her stomach began to flutter with nervousness.

Kamal didn't take his eyes off her, and held out his hand. A customary handshake for all, but the momentary physical contact between the two generated enough electricity to light up the ship. When the contact broke, Rhea felt dazed.

'Hello, Rhea,' he said, his eyes drilling holes into her composure, 'You look lovely!'

She found her throat drying up. 'Thank you,' she replied, forcing the words out. 'You're not looking too bad yourself,' she added softly. He caught it and inclined his head jauntily at her. Then he winked, and her heart nearly stopped. All the days of self-control and steeling herself came to naught.

Naina said something but it drowned in the background noise. Rhea rose to air kiss her, as she complimented her on her look and how the newly acquired tan suited her so much. 'We seem to be at the same table today,' Naina said affably as she settled down in her chair, looking dainty and delicate in a manner Rhea never could. Dressed in a dusty rose gown with discrete embroidery at the décolletage, her dress probably cost more than Rhea's entire income from a single editing project. The evening rolled out with champagne being served, and after the cruise director greeted them all at their tables, the service began. It was particularly hard to refuse the champagne that kept flowing into their glasses, and by the end of the second refill, Rhea found herself happier than she should have been under the circumstances. Naina, who was seated by her side, was even happier.

'Go easy on the champers,' Kamal whispered to Naina on the side. 'You know how it affects you.'

'I'm fine,' she exclaimed, rather too loudly, causing heads in the immediate vicinity to swirl around. The meal was fabulous, not that Rhea could eat much, keenly aware of Kamal sitting barely a few feet away. He kept staring at her occasionally, with the kind of grim faced, questioning look that set her knees trembling and making her unable to concentrate on anything.

'Such a bossy big brother,' Naina said to Rhea over the soup which she was swilling in equal measures with the champagne. 'But he's such a wonderful brother, isn't he?'

Rhea unwittingly looked up to catch Kamal's eyes across the table. For a moment it felt as if everyone at the table could hear her heartbeat.

She decided to turn her concentration on the array of food. Tuna, salmon and shrimp appetizers, lobster bisque, oven-baked fillet of salmon, followed by a delicious tiramisu—Rhea ate everything, and yet tasted nothing. All she was aware of was Kamal, sitting close by and laughing and chatting with some travellers from Australia who were also seated at their table. Each time his eyes settled on her, she felt it physically, like a touch.

Once they were done with their meals, Kamal leaned across to Naina and cut into the conversation, 'I'll just go check on the kids and the babysitter. Will be back in a moment.'

Naina beamed at him with a 100-watt smile and nodded. He strode off with rapid strides that would get him to their cabin in half the time that Naina would take in her high heels. He returned within ten minutes and reported that the kids had raised the right amount of hell and were watching television till their eyes glazed over, but refusing to go to sleep. Naina rolled her eyes, 'They're on holiday too. Let them enjoy themselves, I guess.'

The smaller group at the table decided they would watch a Latin Night performance as billed in their newsletter and trotted off en masse to the auditorium.

Rina Maasi sniffed disapprovingly. 'If I was a little younger and this arthritis hadn't started making my joints misbehave, I could have shown them how it's really done.'

There was a minor discussion amongst the rest of them at the table, confused about what they could move on to from the dinner now concluded.

Luckily, her attention was diverted by the arrival of the Colonel. He looked dapper and she cooed in approval, flagging him to her side and telling Rhea in not so many words that she could now consider herself free to hang out with the younger lot.

'Let's go to the bar,' Naina suggested, 'I feel the need to get totally plastered today and be done with it once on the cruise while we have a babysitter to ensure the kids are tucked in bed.'

Rina Maasi waved them on with her blessings to indulge in hedonistic revelry that would do her proud. 'You young ones, go on, have fun, this wonderful man here will drop me back to the cabin after the show.' Rhea handed over the door key card to her with a strict warning not to forget her night time medications.

Naina was already a little unsteady from the champagne during dinner and balanced herself on Kamal's arm with slow, careful steps. They entered the discotheque to dim lights and loud music. The Colonel's son and his wife were there and had hit the dance floor already, and so did Naina and Kamal, leaving Rhea standing on the fringe of the tiny floor, looking at the crowd and feeling completely alone. Kamal noticed her and beckoned her to join in. Just as she was about to move towards them, someone came crashing on the floor and embraced Rhea in a bear hug. It was John and he definitely had more alcohol flowing in his veins than mandated.

'Where have you been!' he gushed, refusing to let her get out of his embrace. 'Right here, on this ship. Where have you been hiding?' she countered with a pleasant smile, disentangling herself from his arms which had begun caressing her bare back. She stepped back politely and realized that Kamal was looking on.

'Shall we dance?' he asked her, and without waiting for an affirmative response, dragged her into the handkerchief sized dance floor. 'Mmmm, you smell good,' he whispered, drawing her closer to him and nuzzling her neck in a manner that would be considered PG rated in the movies. Rhea felt her back prickle.

But maybe she should loosen up and have some fun, she thought to herself. John looked good—the way the corners of his eyes crinkled into a lattice when he smiled, the tousled, sun bleached golden curls that felt like silk to the touch, the rippled fitness of his body which was sinuous and lithe as it moved to the music, like he really felt the rhythm within him. Perhaps he was just what the doctor ordered to take her mind off depressing thoughts about Samir, and to detach herself from the current obsession with Kamal. They danced for a while when Rhea began to feel that it was enough for the night.

She looked around for Kamal and Naina. They were nowhere to be seen.

'Want to take this party to my cabin? Take up where we left off that night?' John put his arms around her waist, drawing her to him.

She pushed him away gently, but firmly. 'No,' she shook her head. 'Not really.'

'Come on, sweetheart, don't be such a prude,' he said, slipping his hand inside her dress. She moved away from him with a start.

A strong hand grabbed her and pulled her away. 'I'm cutting in on this dance, bro,' Kamal's voice said smoothly.

John shrugged and went back to the floor. As she watched, he started dancing with another woman, the same one he had handed a parcel to, and which she had given to someone at the piazza. The details came floating back to her.

The closed air and the loud music started getting to her. 'You want to go out?' And before she knew it, she was steered out of the discotheque, into the open, salty air of the deck.

Rhea took off her stilettos and stood barefoot, holding her shoes with one hand and grabbing the railing with the other, in a desperate bid to make the world stop swaying. She leaned over the railing precariously, gasping with sudden nausea, and tried to fill her lungs with some fresh air. Never again so much champagne, she reprimanded herself. It didn't suit her. She was better off sticking to cocktails and non-alcoholic drinks.

'Are you all right?' Kamal asked, holding her elbow gently.

'Just a little queasy, but I'll be fine, I just need to get to my cabin.'

He helped her through the post-dinner crowd on the deck, to the elevator bank and down to her deck level. 'I took the liberty of taking your cabin key card from your aunt since I passed her sitting on the promenade deck with the Colonel,' he said as he swiped the door open. 'You were lucky I reached there just in time after dropping Naina to her cabin, or things could have got a little unpleasant with that smooth operator you were dancing with.'

She raised her eyebrows and half turned towards him, bristling with an irritation that was a churning of everything—John, the queasiness from the ship's movement and too much champagne. 'Why are you hell-bent on playing my keeper, Kamal Shahani?' she said, her voice rising a fraction of decibel. 'Why . . . oops . . .' She flung her shoes down on the carpet and ran to the bathroom just as the bile rose in her throat, making it in time to have the vomit hit the rim of the wash basin.

Kamal followed swiftly, holding her hair off her face and stroking her back gently as she spewed all the contents of the dinner, and then washed her face carefully and wiped it with the hand towel. She stood trembling, leaning against the basin for support. He took her by the hand as she moved gingerly to the twin bed she occupied, feeling the room whirl around her. He handed her a glass of water and asked if she needed to see a doctor.

'No,' she insisted, 'I'm fine. Something probably just disagreed with me.'

She lay down, unable to keep her head upright. He pulled the covers up to her neck and stroked her hair gently. 'I'm so embarrassed,' she said softly.

'Don't be,' he replied. 'It was probably the prawn, or the champagne, or both. Now close your eyes and sleep it off. I insist.' She closed her eyes and felt herself drifting off into a void of blackness, a sleep induced by alcohol and giddiness. And that's when she felt it, a kiss on her forehead. 'Sleep well,' he whispered. 'Sleep well, my darling.'

Soft footsteps moved away from her, and then Rhea heard the door close. When she opened her eyes, she was alone in the room. What was happening to her? Why was she irresistibly being drawn to this man who appeared to be completely out of her league?

EIGHT

Rhea woke to Rina Maasi shaking her gently. Her head was still shaky from the dislodged machinery inside from when she had thrown up. Demons were attacking the back of her eyeballs with a hammer, a couple them intent on prying her eyeballs out or inserting red hot pokers into various corners of her cranium.

'Hangover?' Rina Maasi asked pithily.

Rhea nodded ever so slowly, afraid her head would disintegrate if she shook it beyond a millimetre per second.

'Here,' she handed across a glass of water. 'Drink up. You need to hydrate yourself.'

Rhea sat up gingerly, pouring the water down her throat, feeling the water droplets skid and bounce in her bloodstream and then make their way up into her cranium where they began dislodging the hangover demons.

'Never again,' she croaked. 'No champagne.'

'It wasn't the champagne,' Rina Maasi laughed. 'It was the number of glasses you drank. You were tossing them down the hatch like a veteran alcoholic. I quite admired your smooth wrist action.'

Rhea shuddered. Did she do something horrific while she was out of it? The last she could remember was coming into the cabin with Kamal and him holding her hair off her face while she . . . aargggghhhh . . . she vomited in front of him. She cringed at the memory.

'How did you get into the cabin?' she asked.

Kamal had brought the cabin door key back with him and Rina Maasi was informed that she was out of it. 'He insisted I come back immediately because you were unwell. You were fast asleep when I returned.' She nodded gingerly and looked down at herself. She was still in the dress she had worn to dinner and it would now need dry cleaning.

Rina Maasi wasn't quite done with her, though. She insisted Rhea drink some more water and gave her a fizzy antacid to deal with the hangover. 'You need to be careful of how much you drink, my girl. Anything can happen when you are under its influence, surely you don't need me to tell you that. Luckily, Kamal is a gentleman and won't take advantage of a girl who passes out from too much drink. But there's no telling what could have happened if he wasn't around.'

Rhea looked down at her hands, abashed. She felt like a nine-year-old getting a good talking to. 'I won't let myself get drunk again, Rina Maasi. I promise you that. But then, I am on holiday and I am trying to cheer myself up. But, yes, I will watch the alcohol.'

'That's a good girl. Now get up and get ready, we have a shore excursion awaiting us.'

The island of Sicily was the next port of halt. Rhea and Rina Maasi had skipped a couple of shore excursions in the past few days and Rhea had quite enjoyed the quietude of the ship sans the crowds on those days. The pools were empty, the hot tubs didn't have fist fights breaking out in the queues, and the restaurants had enough vacant tables to be allowed a choice of spot.

A pre-booked excursion to the lovely town of Taormina awaited them at Sicily. Rhea was with Rina Maasi, the Colonel and a couple of other retirees from Milwaukee on their mission to go around the world on a cruise ship. Naina and Kamal weren't on their van although Naina had come across to say hello while disembarking and grumbled into Rhea's ear about the telling off she received from her brother about drinking too much the previous night. Rhea hadn't been able to speak to Kamal except for a polite hello and monosyllabic reply to his 'How are you feeling today'. This was followed by an awkward silence when she wondered how to thank him for taking her back to her room and tucking her in. Luckily, Rina Maasi and Naina were too engrossed in conversing with each other to listen to what was being said.

The excursion offered a thankful break to the awkwardness, and the walking tour began by exploring the Greco-Roman amphitheatre which had fabulous views of Mount Etna looming ahead in a strangely macabre way something immensely beautiful, yet dangerous, is. Taormina, a medieval baroque town located snug on the hillside, was not meant for aching arthritic knees since a lot of walking was imperative to get anywhere in the town. Rina Maasi, therefore, gave up the effort in a little while, opting instead to sit and wait for the group to reassemble.

It was also probably a touristy day because the town was packed with visitors. Three cruise liners had docked together and all their passengers had spilled over and into the land, causing the town to seem knee-deep in people.

Rhea's guide, a wonderful Sicilian with earnest black eyes and a mop of shockingly thick black hair, gave them two hours to wander around the place before reassembling right where he had left them. 'You can finish your shopping now!' he announced, gesticulating grandly at the stores along the Corso Umberto where Rina Maasi had already scampered off to despite her bad knee, with the Colonel following suit with an amused expression. He also winced every now and then, indicating that all the walking was putting a strain on his leg.

As Rhea stood there, wondering if she should join her aunt in the stores or wander around on her own, she felt a tug at her handbag and then a slitting noise, followed by the sight of a slight, stocky man running away with her handbag. 'Help, my handbag, stop,' she yelled as loudly as she could and chasing the thief the fastest she could. Before she could reach the man, Kamal, who happened to be in the path the man had taken, grabbed him by the collar, wrestled him to the ground, and retrieved the bag. A couple of locals and the tour guide called excitedly for the police and the petty thief was handed over to the custody of a local constable.

Rhea couldn't stop thanking Kamal. He always seemed to know when she needed help. Perhaps it came from keeping his eye constantly on her. If it wasn't flattering it would have been creepy, she told herself.

She took out her wallet to check for all the cards and money and after putting them back, held on to her handbag as tightly as she could. Unfortunately, one strap had been cut and it hung around aimlessly. There wasn't much money in her wallet, but her identification cards were in it, as well as her bank cards, and replacing all those would have been hell. Her arms and legs were still trembling with the shock, and Rina Maasi rushed from the store she had entered on spotting the commotion outside.

'Are you all right?' she asked, putting her arm around her niece. Rhea nodded, reassuring her aunt that apart from a terrible scare, everything was okay.

'You need to stick to the group,' Rina Maasi said, most annoyed.' Why do you insist on wandering off alone?'

The guide nodded and charmingly explained that while such incidents were rare, they needed to be careful. Kamal, now with Jay hoisted on his shoulders, and Naina with Kiara fell in pace with Rina Maasi and Rhea as they moved down the row of stores in the street.

'Thank you,' Rhea said to him, 'For getting my wallet back, and for taking me back to my cabin yesterday.'

'You don't need to thank me. I did what anyone would have.'

'Well, not many men would escort a drunk woman to her cabin and not take advantage of the situation.'

'How do know I didn't take advantage of you?' he said softly, his eyes fixing themselves on hers. His gaze, when she met it, was softly mocking. 'You were so ready to be taken advantage of.'

She gasped. 'You didn't! I would have known if you had.'

'I didn't. But that is not to say I wasn't sorely tempted to . . .' She gasped again. He laughed.

'Don't you dare!' she said, her cheeks flaming into a brilliant red, realizing the little boy perched on his shoulders was listening in to the conversation with curious ears. 'I told you I'm not looking for a holiday fling.'

'I remember,' he replied, smiling down at her with a look that was both a promise and a caress. 'And I remember replying that neither was I.'

Flustered, she moved away towards where Rina Maasi had entered a shop. 'Rina Maasi,' she called out to her aunt tiredly, 'Maybe what you really need to buy is a huge suitcase to keep all that you have bought already. How on earth are you going to carry everything back on the flight?'

'Don't worry,' she said in the imperious manner she had of one who was used to getting her way. 'I'll find a way.' Rhea shook her head, dreading the haul back—she would have to manage the entire luggage on her own, through the airports, given Rina Maasi's dodgy knee and arthritic hands.

Rhea wasn't buying anything, she barely had enough money to see her through day-to-day, and she had already spent a lot on the wedding that didn't happen. Moreover, she had let go quite a few projects assuming she would be busy with the wedding and honeymoon, and later in setting up her new home. So now she was confronted with the hapless task of drumming up work when she got back. It was terrifying, not having enough money in the bank. Her parents were around, but they lived on pensions which did not extend to lavish handouts to their daughter. The thought of moving back home was scary. Perhaps she could take in a roommate, she told herself. There was space for a bed and a cupboard in the room that she called bedroom, although she valued her privacy and the ability to be completely alone for days if she chose not to see another living being. But now that she was without a full-time job and no reliable source of income, plus a broken engagement, her father might just wash his hands off her.

Nonetheless, she walked along with Naina and Rina Maasi through the shops as they oohed and aahed over jewellery made from the volcanic lava of Mount Etna, the stoles, and artefacts, including the triskelion wall decorations. Triskelion was the symbol of Sicily and Rina Maasi bought quite a few such decorations to gift others back home.

'The problem with going on a trip,' she said as she painstakingly counted out the money after driving Rhea mad by asking her to convert the price into rupees, 'is to bring back enough souvenirs to give away without offending anyone.'

Kamal kept the kids entertained by getting them to chase the errant pigeons fluttering down into the square. On a sugar high since they had consumed more than their mandated level of chocolates, the children were soon tired and bored. 'She hit me', 'He's looking at me, see Mom, see, he's looking at me', were being whined in accusatory tones on a loop.

'I should've tied my tubes when I got married,' Naina mock complained as she deftly fended off the warring factions and kept them close at hand. Kamal hoisted Jay on his shoulders and quelled the squall with that one simple gesture.

'I tell you,' Naina continued, shooting a look of pure gratitude to her brother, 'When you get married, don't have kids. I'm joking of course. Have kids. But space them. Or keep the tranquilizers handy to down with the vodka when it gets too much to handle.'

Her forehead was delicately creased and there were faint purplish dark circles under her eyes. She shushed Kiara who was busy sticking out her tongue at Jay who, in turn, was happily riding on his uncle's shoulders and mocking her back.

'Now kids, if you continue doing that, a bird will swoop down and pluck your tongues out,' Kamal boomed in a valiant effort to restore good behaviour in public. The kids continued whining about perceived favouritism. 'She got to sit at the window', 'He got one extra piece of cake for dessert last night', and so on. They would probably whine about who was allowed to stay in uterus a day longer too, Rhea thought uncharitably, she being an only child and not familiar with this such sibling rivalry. 'He gets to sit on your shoulders all the time,' Kiara sulked.

Rhea walked determinedly a few steps behind them, keenly aware of Kamal's broad shoulders bearing Jay up in front of her, the sturdiness of the way he walked in his sandals and loose cotton trousers and shirt, the looseness doing nothing to conceal the measured perfection of his lean, muscular body.

'Shall we have lunch? I've been surviving on too much gelato all day and my intestines are chilled to ice. I'm sure the kids must be starving too,' Naina said. They were outside a lovely café on the main street with a great sea view and it seemed the most natural thing to do was to sit down, rest their weary feet and refuel. Naina and Rhea ordered some locally made almond wine and wood fire baked pizzas for all. Rina Maasi insisted on some pasta.

'I've already eaten enough on this trip to double up as anchor if the ship loses hers,' Naina confessed with a guilty laugh. There was no evidence of that on her slender frame, Rhea reassured her.

As they ate, Kamal played with the kids, keeping them chortling with laughter while Naina had her meal in peace. Jay went face first into his plate, shovelling in the nutrients with both his hands.

'I finished everything,' he said with pride after a frantic eating spree. 'I can see that,' Kamal replied, glancing at his plate that was clear and sparkling, with the exception of a careful pile of vegetables on one side. Jay then proceeded to chug down a glass of limoncello at breakneck speed.

In this charming restaurant, with the aroma of freshly cooked food thick in the air, she realized how she had actually enjoyed babysitting her younger cousins, she would create games for them to play, and how they waited for her to arrive so they could have a whale of a time. Where had that Rhea disappeared? As she watched Kamal play the mind-numbing game of Stone-Paper-Scissors for the umpteenth time, she wondered what kind of a father Kamal would make. What would it be like to have babies with him? To make babies with him? She squeezed her eyes shut.

Aaarggghhhh! No! She gulped swiftly from her glass. A couple of glasses of wine and she would successfully knock that thought out of her mind. But vague memories of the previous night came flooding back and she decided against more than one glass. She didn't want to repeat her drunk act and have him think of her merely as a lush.

'I wantu go to toilet,' Kiara began whining, all the lemonade pressing on her bladder. Naina marched her firmly to the back of the restaurant and Rina Maasi decided to join them in the queue for the rest room. 'It's a long haul back to the ship and I will not be responsible for myself if I don't get to a restroom immediately,' she laughed.

'Now I wantuhave ice cream,' Jay announced firmly.

Kamal laughed. 'Do you still have place in your stomach for ice cream?' he asked the little fellow.

'There's always place in the stomach for ice cream,' the tyke replied, jutting his chin out in defiance.

Kamal looked at Rhea. 'Would you like some?' he asked.

'No, thanks,' she shook her head to indicate a negative, 'I'm good.'

'Are you sure?' he persisted.

'I am.'

'Then I will eat her share,' Jay interjected.

His was a stubbornness that could not be denied.

'Which flavour do you want,' Kamal asked, and Jay unexpectedly stood up from his chair and groaned a little before heaving out all the contents of his hastily ingested lunch all over the floor.

'And that,' Kamal said as he sat him back on his chair and used a table napkin and a bottle of water to clean him up, 'is what I was afraid of.'

The little fellow had the grace to look exceedingly sheepish and allowed himself to be cleaned up with a firm hand. Kamal looked up at Rhea and smiled, 'I seem to be getting rather good at this.'

She blushed in mortification, but found herself admiring the calmness with which he handled the child.

'Are you okay now, champ?' asked the indulgent and concerned uncle once again. Jay nodded. 'Now sit right here and no ice cream for you until your stomach settles down.'

'Budwai, is nod fair, I finish vomiting now, I'm okay,' Jay began protesting virulently, but was shushed down. 'Because you just threw up all that you had eaten. If you eat anything more, you might bring it up again and we are a long way from the ship and have a long drive back. All I am going to allow you now are juices and water.'

He ruffled his nephew's hair lovingly.

'Okay Kamal Maama. I sit here quietly and be a very good boy.'

'That's my rockstar. And when we get back on the ship, you can eat all the ice cream you want, that's a promise,' Kamal pinched his own throat with his thumb and forefinger in the earnest gesture of the truthful. 'Mother promise.'

'If you don't gimme, Naani will die you know. Den you'll have no mudder.'

Kamal nodded in all seriousness and re-pinched his throat in reiteration.

Rhea couldn't help but laugh out loud at the incongruous gesture. 'Ah, finally, we get some sound out of you. You have been terribly quiet all day,' Rina Maasi announced her return to the table. Looking around she declared that she must shop some more before their free time was up. The Colonel, who was nose deep into his third pint of beer, rose gallantly, offering to escort her to the stores down the street despite the rather pronounced limp that was definitely the result of a sore leg stump from all the walking around they had done since morning.

'Want to come along with us, Rhea?' she asked, a mere formality, given she was already on her way, 'I know you detest shopping, so don't feel obliged to come just to make an old lady happy.'

Rhea shook her head. 'I'll just wait here for you, Rina Maasi, I really have nothing to shop for.' Except, perhaps, that one ring, she had spotted, tried on and kept back because she really couldn't allow herself that indulgence. Samir had given her an engagement ring that had a couple of small diamonds set on it. After the fiasco, she flushed it down the toilet in anger. Without thinking, her right hand went to the spot where the ring used to be and she circled its invisible shadow. The emptiness on that finger once again reminded Rhea that she was no longer part of a couple, that Samir, whom she had begun to consider as a solid presence in her life was no longer part of it, and that she was all alone. Her skin drained itself of colour.

Kamal cast a quizzical look at the mock twirling of a phantom ring on her left hand. 'I hope you are well and not going to hurl out your lunch too?'

'I'm fine,' she replied, still embarrassed about the previous night. 'Don't worry about me.'

He raised an eyebrow and half-smiled. 'I won't,' he replied and turned towards Jay who was now raring to get back to running around at warp speed and knocking down innocent bystanders who happened to get in his way. Naina bustled back to the scene with a grumpy Kiara who had obviously had an accident with a faucet or the wash basin because the front of her dress was soaking wet. 'Just the day I forget to pack along a change of clothes, look what she goes and does,' Naina grumbled to no one in particular. Kamal laughed. 'Don't bother, it will dry soon enough. And by the way, Jay just vomited all he ate.'

Naina gasped and hurried to the little fellow who had found himself a comfortable spot on a bench outside the restaurant. Dangling his legs merrily, he surveyed everything around like a king.

'Are you alright? What happened? Are you feeling sick now?' his mother enveloped him in her arms and in a pile of questions.

He brushed off the maternal concern with an airy wave of his hand, 'I am okay now and I want ice cream.'

Rhea interrupted despite herself, 'Give the boy his ice cream Kamal. At the worst, he'll hurl it up again.'

Kamal turned slowly to look at her. His gaze burned a hole into her eyes but she couldn't understand his expression. 'If you insist, I will, but first young man, your mother has to tell me it is okay.'

'Mamma,' Jay whined, 'Please can I have ice cream?'

The indulgent mother erred on the side of caution. 'When we get back to the ship, perhaps, but I would like some, Kamal.'

As Kamal rose from his chair and took a step towards the gelato counter, Jay pulled him back by his trouser and beckoned him to bend down to his eye level.

'Is this the aunty you are getting married to?' Jay's eyes were earnest and enquiring as his finger pointed with no sense of restraint at Rhea, who in turn felt her cheeks go ablaze with a furiously embarrassed blush.

'No, of course not,' Kamal said in a brusque, clipped tone. 'Whatever gave you that idea?'

Jay cocked his head and continued unabashedly, 'Because when she tole you to ged me ice cream, you agreed. You never lissen to mamma or naani.'

'Well, you got that wrong, young man. I was just feeling sorry for you because you were sick. Now, don't worry too much about who I am getting married to.'

'But naani is always being worried about when you will marry to an aunty. And she said she hoped you weren't thinking of marrying that snake. Why were you marrying a snake, Kamal Maama?'

'I'm not marrying anyone, champ, snake or human,' Kamal said patiently. 'Let's have a deal. You choose who I should get married to, okay?'

'Okay, marry to this aunty, she is priddy and I like her,' Jay replied in an instant.

Kamal laughed aloud before striding away briskly to get the gelato. Rhea stood rooted to the spot, embarrassed at the conversation that took place right in front of her.

Naina broke in apologetically. 'I'm sorry about that. Kids, you know, they come up with the most random statements. Please don't mind.'

'Of course not,' Rhea replied. She sighed and looked into the distance where Kamal was standing at a stall. He entered a small shop, the one she had visited along with Naina a short while ago.

'He doesn't discuss anything with us, neither with my mother, nor with me. He's reserved that way,' Naina continued about her brother. 'But I know the girl Jay referred to as "snake". She's actually a family friend, a lovely girl, but I don't know what went wrong between the two of them. Amid all that confusion, I returned home. My divorce came through and as you can imagine I really needed a break, to get away from everything for a while. So, here we are. Perhaps this is a getaway that he needed too.' She stopped at this point and gave Rhea a quick and assessing gaze that made her go red all over again. 'Please don't let him know I discussed this with you, he will get mad with me. But I would hate to see him get into any casual relationship just as a rebound. He is a good guy. He deserves a good woman.'

Was that a warning to stay away from her brother, Rhea wondered. Was that Naina's way of telling her to keep off?

'I'm sure he does,' she replied, non-committal, as the man being discussed strolled back with two ice creams in his hands.

The tour guide rounded them up. Rina Maasi clambered on the bus happily, carrying a bag packed with carefully wrapped ceramic masks that she had set her eyes on and telling everyone how she got a good deal and that no matter where in the world you were, you should never be ashamed to bargain. 'I've kept the ugliest one for your mother and I will insist she puts it up in the living room,' she laughed at the thought and then continued kindly, 'So did you have a good time today?' patting Rhea's knee as she sat next to her on the bus.

'Yes, I did Rina Maasi,' Rhea replied dutifully, unwilling to tell her that her heart was still broken and that she had torn it apart some more by falling for this infuriatingly handsome man with a chiselled jaw and questioning eyes.

By the time they reached the ship, the sun was low on the horizon and it was time to cast off from the port they were anchored at. As they moved onto the vessel, their feet became weary, and the two children slept in the arms of their mother and uncle. Just then a cry, 'Kamaaaal!' rang through the air.

Kamal stopped in his tracks. Naina turned around slowly and so did Rhea. Running towards them was perhaps the most beautiful woman Rhea had ever seen in her life.

'Sonia . . .' Naina said, breaking the silence that descended on the company upon seeing this vision in their midst. 'Fancy seeing you here!'

Sonia threw her head back and laughed merrily. 'Yes, fancy seeing me here. It took some organizing but I could finally catch up with you and board the ship here.'

She looked familiar and Rhea could finally place her. Sonia Mehrotra, a well known face in the Mumbai society pages, a patron of the arts, an occasional fashion designer, and hailing from an old, wealthy family. Naina remembered her manners and did the introductions gracefully.

'Soni Ma'am, Rhea, Colonel Singh, meet Sonia, Kamal's girlfriend. Sonia, this is Soni Ma'am, Kamal's school headmistress, her niece Rhea, and Colonel Singh from Chandigarh.'

They smiled politely at each other and Rhea managed to say her 'Hello, pleased to meet you' in a normal tone without revealing the sudden churning that was occurring in her intestines.

Kamal, having now transferred the sleeping Jay to his other arm, spoke looking directly at Rhea, 'Actually, she's now my ex-girlfriend.'

NINE

Rina Maasi entered the cabin and collapsed on her bed, exhausted and drained. 'Can you imagine, Kamal has also gone through a break-up. This ship is full of young people with broken hearts,' she sighed. Rhea made a face. She was glad when her aunt announced she was going to take a nap.

Rhea didn't know how to process this sudden turn of events. Sonia was glamorous and she realized that she was far from being remotely in the league of women Kamal had dated. She went into the shower—an icy cold shock was what was required to calm the chaotic thoughts in her head and steer away the exhaustion of the day. She let the icy needles of water pound her bare skin for a good ten minutes before she shifted the lever directions to make the water scalding hot. She lathered herself up and felt the tiredness of the day sluice off with the dust and grime. As she towelled herself down, she caught a glimpse of herself in the mirror. It was not something she did easily—examine her naked reflection.

A long and lean figure looked back. Rhea had grown up being called matchstick by less charitable classmates, but as she filled out a little in college, she had to fend off modelling agents hanging around the college campus, enticing her to come for auditions. She had no illusions about her appearance—she was attractive, but nowhere close to the stunning ex-girlfriend of Kamal's. Sonia was all curves and breathtaking views, designed to give unwary men a dislocation in their necks as she passed. Her eyes were almond shaped and of a particularly molten shade of brown, her skin was of tawny gold perfection, her lips were full and sensuous, her cheekbones sharp.

Rhea, on the other hand, was too lean for her own liking and would have liked to have some curves. Samir had always grumbled how both her breasts put together weren't quite enough to fill his hands. All the rush she felt when Jay insisted Kamal marry her because she was 'priddy' evaporated with the steaming vapour from the shower. She couldn't see herself anymore, the mirror was now foggy.

Rhea kicked the steel wastepaper basket placed beneath the basin in a moment of sheer overpowering pique. She rubbed the mirror and looked at her face again, dissecting every feature and comparing it unfavourably to Sonia. Her nose, she decided, was too sharp and seemed pointed in certain unflattering angles. In fact, an unwary person who dashed against her could be impaled by it. Her lips were too wide, took up the better part of the lower half of her face, and sometimes pouted on their own accord. Her eyes were the best part of her, she decided. They were black and were of the variety that some folks called big. She was justifiably vain about her eyes and regularly invested in every eye pencil and mascara that was launched in the market to emphasise them. Her standard look was simple—kohl lined eyes, a bit of mascara, and a slick of lip gloss. Sonia, who looked like she had been professionally made up for a photo shoot, made her realize just how inadequate her make-up routine was.

A sudden, scary thought hit her. Was Naina's remark about gold diggers targeted at her? After all, she was definitely working class. Her clothes were a mix of high street brands and flea market shopping. She was from a different world. Kamal was completely out of her league and she was silly to think otherwise. She pulled herself up and decided: she would go back to Delhi, stick a knife into each of Samir's car tyres, and set about rebuilding her life as a strong, independent woman.

She stuck her tongue out at her reflection and went out into the cabin. Pulling on a pair of shorts and a T-shirt, she let her wet hair dry out naturally rather than the smoothened perfection she was getting used to seeing it in. She didn't apply her regular lip gloss, nor the kohl pencil as was her norm after bathing. Rina Maasi, who was done with her short nap and was pouring herself some tea, looked at Rhea and raised a questioning brow.

'In mourning, are we?' she asked.

'Ha ha. No, just too tired to dress up for dinner now. Can we skip going to the dining hall and order in?'

Rina Maasi nodded. Her feet were stretched out and resting on the foot stool, and she cast an agonized look at them.

'Sounds good. I am too tired to take another step anyway. I wish I could soak my feet in hot water with some salts. Did you get a good look at the girl who was all over Kamal?' Rina Maasi asked, and continued without waiting for a response. 'Any more spillage from her top and an outfielder could have taken a catch. And the make-up? I'm sure she is a few kilos lighter after she cleanses it off.'

Rhea laughed. 'Don't be mean, Maasi, she is very pretty.'

'Plastic,' Maasi said dismissively. 'Probably non-recyclable and hazardous to the environment as well. Don't like her.'

'You barely said hello to her,' Rhea laughed. 'It isn't enough to dislike her.'

'Just the vibes that came off her . . . a really smug, look-at-me vibe,' Rina Maasi insisted. 'I've seen enough of these glamazons amongst the mothers of the kids at school. They have so much work done on them that if near a candle, they could catch fire! Do you think that pert nose came genetically to her? It probably came with a three for two offer on the breasts and the lips.'

Rhea roared with laughter. Rina Maasi was incorrigible, but thanks to her, the mood lightened up instantly.

'She was dating a freshly divorced industrialist scion. I remember seeing them together on the party pages. I don't know when the "Kamal's girlfriend" bit came about . . .' she felt her voice crack and heart sink as she said it.

'Don't believe everything you read in the newspapers, child,' Rina Maasi said gently, throwing a concerned glance at Rhea's woebegone face. 'And he did say ex-girlfriend, if I remember correctly. But then why should it matter to you, whether she is an ex-girlfriend or not? I hope you are not falling for him?'

'Of course not,' Rhea replied with a vehemence she did not feel. And that was the end of that discussion.

They ordered a meal and tucked into it heartily with the appetite that comes from a day's worth of tiredness. Rhea was tired but not sleepy and felt like a little walk to settle her jangled nerves.

'I think I'll step out on the deck for a little stroll. Would you like to join me, Rina Maasi?' Rhea asked out of courtesy, but not really wanting the company.

'You go on ahead, child. I'm going off to sleep.' Rina Maasi was frantically changing channels on the television, trying to find a news channel with clear reception and grumbling about the state of the world where an old lady is deprived of her daily dose of news viewing.

Some instructions later about storing her purchases of the day properly so that the ceramic didn't get cracked, Rhea stepped out and into the passage, taking the elevator to the Promenade Deck where there would be enough people strolling around after dinner, trying to get their digestive systems to accept the hedonism of the meal just eaten.

It was a pleasant Mediterranean summer night. The starry sky above, a smooth promenade below, the gently lapping waves around the ship, and a soft breeze that played with her hair. She smiled at a couple of familiar faces—a few days on the ship and the army of retired folks and families were now acquaintances.

After a complete round of the promenade, Rhea stood at a relatively deserted spot, stern-side, trying to sort out the confusion of her thoughts whirling into each other. The sudden softening in her heart when she saw Kamal handling a young child who was unwell, the fluttering in her stomach when Jay asked him if Rhea was the lady he planned to marry and, the fierce disappointment when he dismissed it. And finally, the wave of fiery, stabbing jealousy when Naina introduced Sonia as Kamal's girlfriend.

'Get a grip on yourself, Rhea,' she spoke to herself in the sternest tones she could muster. 'You barely know the man. A few days together on the ship and a back massage does not make him the next love of your life.'

But a sudden plummeting feeling in her chest told her it didn't feel like the next love of her life—it felt like it was the only time she had ever been so exquisitely, tinglingly aware of a man's presence. He surrounded her, either with his presence or with his thoughts. She buried her head in her hands, trying to drive away the images crowding her mind of Kamal and Sonia close together. She shook her head and closed her eyes. Sonia was gorgeous. She was also, obviously, from a similar social background as Kamal was. They made a suitable, good-looking couple. Rhea needed to have a chat with Priya, her best friend in the whole wide world, to sort out her thoughts but needed to find the cyber café which was somewhere on this very deck.

Priya was wise beyond her years. She was married with a child and knew just when Rhea was about to collapse into a puddle of self-inflicted misery and could snap her out of it.

She was the first person Rhea had called when she received the damned email from Samir, bailing out on her and the wedding. Her first reaction? 'Good. Now go sell his ring and get yourself some other jewellery instead.' Of course, Rhea didn't listen to her sound advice.

She decided to check if Priya was online and Skype with her. Perhaps the cyber café on board was still open . . . if she wasn't mistaken, it was somewhere alongside the main promenade. She turned around, peering into the lit windows of the restaurants, bars and lounges in hope of finding it. Unsuccessful, she realized that she needed the deck map instead of wandering around. She stopped short in her tracks when she spotted Sonia and Kamal waiting at the elevator bank. Sonia had her arm tucked into Kamal's and he was making no effort to withdraw it. Rhea stood still, watching, not realizing that she was clearly visible.

Sonia, talking animatedly, put her head down on Kamal's shoulder and continued saying something Rhea couldn't hear. Kamal's face was unreadable, his eyes were fixed firmly on the elevator indicator button. 'Ex-girlfriend, my foot!' Rhea thought with an overwhelmingly juvenile desire to stamp the foot on the ground.

They looked cosy together and very made-for-each-other perfect, she thought. Looking down at her shorts, T-shirt and sandals clad self, Rhea felt unsophisticated in front of Sonia's bandage dress that emphasized her ripe fullness instead of containing it. Rina Maasi was right, she thought in a mean moment, there was enough silicon in that chest to run supercomputers. She was still in the middle of her thoughts when Sonia turned to her side and looked directly at Rhea, standing there frozen. A split second later, Kamal's eyes looked in the same direction. Sonia smiled pleasantly at her and Kamal looked suddenly worried as if he had been caught in the act. Rhea smiled back and scuttled away.

'Gosh, you absolute ninny,' she smacked herself metaphorically on the forehead, 'You look like some sad stalker, trawling the ship to follow him.'

She felt the blood rush to her face and walked as fast as she could. Only when she reached the other end of the ship did she stop, chest heaving with the exertion, limbs trembling with embarrassment and cheeks flaming with shame of being caught staring at two people she shouldn't have been watching at all.

Just then her phone rang, jangling her already shredded nerves. Who would call her in the midst of a cruise, she thought, and she was damned if she was going to pay the international roaming rate to take a call from a telemarketer while looking down to check who it was. She looked down . . . it was flashing a name she least expected to see. Samir. Rhea dropped down on a conveniently placed deck chair right behind her and looked at the screen again, numb.

It stopped ringing after a while. Then the phone vibrated, indicating she had a message. With trembling hands, she slid the homescreen open to check. Samir.

'Can v talk? Am so so sorry, I was stupid. I love u. Can we forget this happened and get back together? It was all a big mistake.'

Then another buzz. 'Please call me. I want to meet you. I know you're not in India, but I am waiting for you.'

Another one.

'I love you, Ree. I want you back. I panicked. I was being selfish, stupid. Forgive me.'

And more.

Finally, an email that must have been in drafts, given it would have taken quite a while to type out his explanation of suddenly panicking at the thought of being married and how he was a cad, and a cur and she had every right to hate him. She scanned the messages and the email over and over again, trying to read more into them than the words themselves. Had he been drunk when he typed them out? How did he know she was not in town, had he visited her home? And more importantly, whatever happened to the bounteous beauty he had escaped to Bali with; had a couple of weeks in her company overwhelmed him already? Could he not deal with his palms being overfull?

Her hands began to quiver. This was what she had prayed for. But now Rhea wasn't sure. She put her phone by her side on the chair and buried her head in her hands. What should she do? Should she call him back, take him back, go back home and get married to him? He was familiar, tried and tested, so to say. Her parents had approved of him—he was a tick against every mandatory box in their list for an ideal son-in-law: decent family, well educated, a good job and a non-smoker. And they liked the fact that Rhea would stay in the same city, at least while Samir was posted there.

'I should reply,' she told herself. 'I should at least tell him I need time.' There was a sudden visceral terror of letting him get away the second time and taking the risk of being alone for the rest of her life.

The calmer, more rational part of her, however, stopped the crazy panicking and took deep, calming breaths. 'Let me not do anything in a rush,' she continued her self-conversation.

'Let me speak to someone, Priya, or Rina Maasi. Someone, anyone.'

She sat back waiting for a long time, both to collect her thoughts as well as to avoid bumping into Kamal and Sonia at the elevator bank. She wanted to return to her cabin without embarrassing herself any further. Rina Maasi would be asleep now, she guessed. She would show her these messages in the morning and then decide what was to be done with them. She needed to sleep, perhaps the answers would be clear in the morning.

TEN

Walking back slowly, Rhea decided to read the messages from Samir again. Was there something she was missing in that sudden barrages of texts and emails? She stopped at a deserted part of the deck and began scrolling through her WhatsApp again. He seemed genuinely contrite. She gripped the railing hard, making her knuckles go white and rocked herself on the balls of her feet, letting the motion distract her. This part of the deck was usually dark, being practically unused by the public. It led to the service areas and had a couple of chairs, just in case someone wanted to rest their feet, but at this hour it was absolutely empty. It suited her, the dark cloak of blackness. She didn't need to smile at passing familiar faces, didn't need to ask them how their day had been.

Rhea stood, quiet and tense, re-living the horrible moment when Kamal looked right at her, his face a mixture of shock and horror. He was probably wondering how long she had been standing there, spying on them. 'But I wasn't spying,' she told herself. 'I just happened to be there . . . but they don't know that. God, I hope he doesn't think I was following them around.' She shuddered at the thought. And then there were the messages sent by Samir. How did she land herself in so much confusion?

She pulled out a tissue from her messenger sling pouch and mopped her face of the cold, clammy sweat. Sipping some water from the bottle she had carried along, Rhea sat back on the chair and stretched her legs.

It was a beautiful, balmy night. The breeze played gently with her hair, the slow rise and fall of the ship was soporific. She closed her eyes and felt time pass by uncertainly. Perhaps if she stayed on her problems would vanish. Voices drifted over the sea breeze, carrying up to her from a lower deck. One of the voices was familiar. John. She would recognize his husky smooth tone anywhere.

'The divers will take the crate with the stash when we dock at port, but I have word that the boss wants one packet to be delivered into town by a mule before he okays the consignment.'

Rhea's ears pricked up. The voice that replied was hushed and unfamiliar, even then she could hear what was being said. The 'mules' discussed were not of the four legged beasts of burden variety, but drug peddlers! She stifled a gasp. 'Never, ever eavesdrop,' her mother's well meaning words, delivered as part of the standard good behaviour lecture, came back to her. 'Nothing good comes of it.'

But this seemed to be too tempting a conversation not to eavesdrop upon, and she packed her qualms in the back pocket of her conscience and continued listening intently. 'The last one got delivered okay, but I can't ask the same person to deliver another one,' John said.

'What is this new obsession with sending packages to people in town? It gets risky, all I agreed to was to accompany the stuff and ensure that it got off-loaded. Why aren't they hiring the oldies to cart the stuff onshore anymore?'

'The customs are alert about the old folk now. Too many of them have been used. This quarter kilo is like a token, or a sample to the deal. It is for the tasting and checking before it gets paid for or collected. If the stuff is okayed, the divers will come in sometime in the night and take the consignment from the hull.'

'Twenty kilos?' John asked, his voice hushed and reverential.

'Yes,' replied the other voice. 'Twenty kilos. All in baby food jars, sealed and packed.'

'Mother of Christ, what I could do if I had it in my hand!'

'It is infinitely better that you don't have it in your hand. Just make sure you hand the small package quickly to someone else to carry into port. Don't choose a retired person, they check them more carefully since the last time we had a consignment seized from that nice old lady with the white curls from Somerset.'

'Oh yes,' John whistled in what seemed to be relief. 'Thank God I didn't give her my real name and slipped off the ship when I saw her being stopped by the customs.'

'By the way, what is your real name?' asked the other voice.

'You don't need to know it. I think I've forgotten it myself.'

'You dawg.'

The image of John handing over a small package to the lady at the disembarkation queue and the lady handing it across to the swarthy faced smoothie in the piazza flashed back in Rhea's mind. The jigsaw puzzle began to slide into place. Disused cogs and cranks in her brain circuitry clicked and whirred as she began putting things together.

She stood up from the chair, careful to remain in the shadow, and peered over to look at the deck below. There was a dim light illuminating the spot where the two men stood. Like the place she was standing in, that area too was right at the rear of the ship and was isolated. 'Do you have an alternative?'

'Yes,' John replied. 'An elderly lady from India, a retired school headmistress, and her niece are travelling on this ship. I think I've charmed the niece enough to get her to willingly agree to take a small package for me off ship. Do you have it ready?'

'Yes,' replied the other man. Rhea peeped over the railing to see a balding, middle-aged, innocuous looking man in crew uniform. 'Two fifty grams of the purest stuff. Hope your softened-up one doesn't open it and start snorting.'

They were discussing her! Rhea's heart gave a thump that she was sure was audible all the way down to the lower deck.

'Do you have a photograph of this girl? How will they recognize her?'

'Will send it across. She's quite a piece.'

'Have you got into her knickers yet?'

'Almost did, but she's very prickly. Would rather not risk her going off me completely.'

'I can't believe it,' the crew member said, 'You seem to have a knack for getting these women into bed! Apart from the fact that you have a full head of hair, I don't understand what your charm is.'

John laughed softly, a laugh that had no humour and was chillingly menacing.

'I listen to them, that's all I do. And all they want is for someone to pay them attention.'

'I'll have the package dropped in at your cabin the night before we dock.' They were scheduled to dock a day away.

'Done, mate.'

They back thumped each other in a typical testosterone fuelled male manner and went their opposite ways. Rhea sank back into her chair. What she had unwittingly overheard was dynamite information that she needed to bring to the ears of the right authorities. If this was indeed a ring of professional narcotic smugglers, she wanted no truck of it. Some countries had limbs and body parts loped off and some sent you straight to the firing squad, some kept you incarcerated till you became the living dead and all consular interventions were hopeless. She didn't know what the laws in this part of the world were, given that they were sailing between Italy and Spain now, but she didn't want to find herself on the other side of it. Of course, she could just refuse to carry the parcel, but to know about an impending wrongdoing and not do anything about it made her uncomfortable.

'What should I do? Who can I ask about what should I do?' she wondered.

There was no one on board she could trust to handle this information with the maturity it deserved. 'Perhaps I should just go to the Captain. But why would he listen to me, he might think I'm just making it up.' For one wild moment she thought of going to Rina Maasi, but the thought of her excitable nature made her stop. It wasn't a good idea. Rina Maasi would hunt John down with the riding crop she threatened her students with and alert the entire ship to the fact that her niece was being recruited as a drug mule. She wouldn't be able to live with that kind of an embarrassment.

She could tell the Colonel, but he might just tell Rina Maasi and she would get an earful for mixing up with the wrong sort of men, and never hear the end of it.

She needed someone cool, calm and sensible. Someone who could be trusted to not fly off the handle and think of a sensible option. There was only one such person she knew on the ship. Kamal. She could talk to him about it. He would know what to do. Rhea knew she could count on him, she had never been surer in her life.

And, of course, there was a small corner of her heart which wanted to see him to explain that contrary to what it looked like, she had not been stalking him. It had just been an unhappy coincidence that she was standing there when they appeared in front of her.

The watch on her wrist showed it was a little after midnight, time for most people to take themselves and their blistered feet to bed. She gave her stomach a few minutes to settle down after overhearing the conversation before rising to her feet and padding along gently towards the elevator bank. There were phones on the side of the alcove that allowed one to ring to the cabins directly. Rhea picked one up and without any hesitation dialled Kamal's cabin number. She had memorized the number to heart after innocuously asking Naina how was it that she and Kamal were on different decks. Kamal answered on the second ring, his voice dull and strained.

'Hello,' she said, her voice faint.

'Rhea?' his voice lifted into a barely concealed joyousness.

Her knees liquefied to jelly and she sagged against the wall. He sounded like he had been expecting her call.

'Kamal,' she said and realized that the conversation had to go further than taking each other's names.

'I need to speak with you urgently.'

'Me too,' he replied. What did he need to speak to her about? Rhea's stomach lurched uncomfortably, but this was not queasiness. It was in anticipation of a touch, the feel of his hands on her body, moving, stroking, evoking more sensations than would be considered legal.

'I can't talk over the phone . . .' she said hesitantly.

'Tell me where you are, I'll come there.'

'I don't think we can talk about this on the deck. I can't risk us being overheard and we can't talk about it in my cabin because Rina Maasi must be asleep. It's . . . it's something dangerous,' her voice dropped to a whisper and she cradled the phone like a baby.

'Well, then, there is only one option. Come to my cabin.'

He put the phone down with a definite click. Wondering if she was doing the right thing, Rhea pressed the button for the elevator. Amid all other thoughts she cursed herself for not applying even a speck of kohl to her eyes. Dressed in a T-shirt and shorts that she normally sleeps in, Rhea felt under dressed. No chance he's going to feel the hots for you, girl; you look like something the cat dragged in after the dog regurgitated it, she told herself bitterly. Just as well, she wasn't going in for the romance anyway.

She buzzed the door of Kamal's cabin hesitantly. It was opened in an instant, almost as if he was standing right at the door, waiting for her to show up. He stood aside politely, gesturing for her to walk in. She entered, looking around, trying to ascertain details of him by his immediate surroundings. She gathered two things immediately, that he was a reader of good fiction and that he was messy. The first cancelled out the second.

There was a book kept face down. *The Great Gatsby*! She looked at him with renewed respect. But this was not the time to talk about Daisy and Jay and doomed, unrequited love. There was drugs, smuggling, and her possible recruitment as a drug mule to be discussed. The room was messy, clothes thrown on the backs of chairs, iPads and laptops on the unmade bed, all available sockets being used to charge gadgets, an open suitcase and its clothes in a chaos after a seemingly frantic ruffle to find what was required. The neatness OCD in her shuddered and gave up the ghost quietly. She could never understand how people could not keep their immediate surroundings neat and tidy. More importantly, how could she find such a person attractive—she, who would go bonkers even if a picture was placed askew in her house?

He stepped back and closed the door behind with a slight click. Rhea stood still, barely millimetres away from him, inhaling his strong musky fragrance. Kamal was in a pair of shorts and a thin cotton T-shirt, evidently getting ready to go to bed.

In the unflattering fluorescent light, she saw his pupils dilate visibly, almost as if he was drinking in the sight of her. She looked at him with desire coursing through her veins.

'Are you all right?' he asked in a concerned voice as he saw her sway a little, unaided by inebriating spirits of course, but he didn't know that.

'One minute, please,' she said, raising her hand up slightly. 'I'm sorry, I just need to visit the bathroom urgently.'

He extended a hand graciously, directing her towards it. She rushed in, closed the door and put her palms to her burning cheeks, staring at her reflection in the mirror. She looked like she had walked off the sets of Zombie Apocalypse. She splashed water on her face, squeezed out some toothpaste on her finger, jabbed it around her mouth and rinsed it out, telling herself it wasn't like she was expecting some nooky, but it was good to be safe.

When she emerged, he was seated on the single arm chair, leaving the entire sofa free for her. She sat primly in the centre, wondering what was the appropriate per foot distance rule to keep with men who one found terribly attractive but had no intention of getting involved with.

'I needed to talk to you about something,' she began.

He cocked his head to the side.

'First of all, I wasn't spying or stalking Sonia and you, I just happened to be there at that point, behind the two of you.'

He broke the smouldering look with a sardonic smile. 'I'm heartbroken. I thought you were going to challenge Sonia to a fist fight. It has always been my fantasy to have two women fighting over me.' And looking at her shocked expression, he laughed out loud.

'Of course you weren't spying on us! I spotted you ambling up and down the promenade much before you saw us.'

She breathed a deep sigh of relief. 'I was mortified that you thought I was . . .' His eyes were so lovely, she realized, as she stopped mid-sentence and looked deep into them. 'Now,' he interjected smoothly, 'What was the "second of all" thing you wanted to talk with me about? I am sure you had something else, other than this, to want to meet me so urgently and under such secretive circumstances.'

She nodded and gave him the low down of the conversation she had overhead. He listened and nodded at appropriate places. At the end of her narrative, he got up and paced the small room, which, because of the arrangement of unnecessary tables and sofas and a rather inviting bed, ended up being a three step pace and turn.

'There's only one solution I can think of—you need to take this to the ship's authorities.'

'I thought of that too, but I am terrified. If they find out I ratted on them, they will slit my throat in my sleep. Or poison my entrée and I will collapse face first in the soup. Or they will tie a stone to my legs and throw me overboard.'

He laughed, but his face was grim. 'I'm sure none of that will happen. The authorities will take care of that.'

She stood up. 'How can that be possible? Someone will get to know that I spilled the beans. I will get a horse head on my bed, followed by a stiletto blade stuck between my shoulder blades.'

His gaze dropped unwittingly to her shoulders. 'It would be tough to smuggle a horse head on board, dripping blood, and I couldn't let that happen to those lovely shoulders, could I?' he said, his voice soft. 'Who will I apply sun block on if something were to happen to those shoulders?'

The vagaries of wearing a wide, boat necked T-shirt had ensured that one of the shoulders referred to was now enticingly bare and exposed. He took a step closer to her, put his hand out and lifted her to her feet, bending towards the exposed shoulder and kissing it softly, from the nape of her neck to the clavicle. She felt herself melt into molten longing and despite herself, pulled him closer to her and let his lips wander further down her shoulders. Her hands went of their own volition, to the skin below his T-shirt, moving over the taut, rippled abdomen, feeling the muscles tense at her touch, the skin smooth as silk below her fingers. He groaned.

She closed her eyes and felt moistness in the hidden places where it ached for him. He drew her to him and pressed his body into hers, making no excuses for the fact that he was aroused. His breathing was heavy and ragged. His hands opened the button on her shorts and began reaching down, she could feel a throbbing begin in spots that went by a letter from the alphabet, reputed to be hard to reach.

'No, no,' she dragged out every ounce of self-control and gently pushed him away.

His eyes were heavy. 'No?' he asked thickly, drawing her to him and letting her feel how her proximity was affecting him, the desire in his eyes echoing the reaction of his body.

'No,' she repeated firmly.

She was proud of her stalwart resistance in the face of such knee-shaking persuasion as he leaned in and kissed her again.

'No.' This stuck record dialogue was not moving the plot along much.

He breathed deeply and moved back. 'No.'

For a moment they stood like statues, each afraid to move for fear they would reach out and undo what massive amounts of self-control had made possible.

'Never let it be said that I forced my attention on a woman saying no.'

There was a heavy silence between them.

He rubbed his forehead with a weary hand and turned his back towards her. She sat down on the sofa, unsure if her legs would hold her. 'There is only one thing to be done right now,' he said, his voice still slightly thick, rubbing a weary hand across his eyes.

'And what is that?'

'We need to get the hell out of this cabin before we do something we both regret and go find the Captain to tell him what you just overheard.'

ELEVEN

It took some convincing for the polite woman manning the twenty-four hour guest services desk to agree that they needed to speak to the Captain urgently. Her perfectly made up face barely changed its neutral expression as she listened to their story, and only when Kamal insisted that it had something to do with the security of the ship that a few buttons were pressed on the intercom and words were spoken in a hushed tone to a disembodied voice at the other end.

Two burly security officers entered the area and indicated that Kamal and Rhea were to follow them. They went through a warren of lifts and passages until they finally emerged into a large conference room. They were asked to wait. Kamal kept pacing the floor while Rhea sat on a chair, acutely aware of each of his movement although he was behind her.

Exactly twenty minutes later, the Captain, a Danish man in his mid-fifties, breezed in. Rhea liked him instantly. He had a no-nonsense attitude, tempered pleasantly with a warm smile, which was encouraging, given the fact that he must have had a long day. He was accompanied by a couple of more men from his team and greeted both of them politely by their names.

'So,' he said, sitting back in a chair, 'What is this matter you needed to urgently communicate to us, madam?'

Rhea outlined the conversation she had overheard earlier once again, repetition adding to the details she had initially forgotten.

On her mentioning that divers would be used to get at the contraband, he gasped in shock and drew out a wireless phone to make a hushed call, punctuated with minimal gesturing. Some orders were barked out to the men accompanying him and they, in turn, went out to execute them, sending other uniformed men in.

'Could you describe the crew member you saw in conversation with this man, John?' Passenger charts were already called for and it was found that the cabin she said John was occupying was booked under the name of Jonathon Merritt. A quick scan of the passenger profile confirmed it was him. A run through of all the cameras on the deck showed the footage of both the offending parties emerging at around the same time from opposite ends of the deck. However there was none to show them conversing, and therefore there was no proof that they had been talking to each other.

Within minutes, the Coast Guard was alerted about their scheduled arrival and the possibility of needing to secure the port. A wait and watch alert was also sounded amongst select members of the crew and after a much hushed and animated discussion, a plan was formulated that needed Rhea's cooperation. For all its worth, she felt like a Bond girl after hearing her role.

'My brave young lady,' said the very dignified Captain, taking a seat opposite hers and holding one of her hands his. 'We need you to draw this man out with the contraband and we need to grab him with the contraband on his person. For this you need to be very careful, meet him, agree to carry the package, fix a spot to meet him in order to collect the package and then when he arrives to meet you, we will swoop in.'

She nodded.

'Any doubts, any queries?'

'Will he hand it to me? Will I be around while he is being arrested?'

'Yes,' said the chief security officer, a burly man in uniform who she knew from the introductions on the first formal night on the ship. 'But we don't know if he is or will be armed, or what sort of back up they have on the vessel; if there are more members on board who would provide cover during the parcel exchange. So we will move in immediately, you don't need to worry, we will ensure you are safe. We just recommend you stay on board and don't do the shore excursion if he has sent your photograph to his contacts on shore.'

'I'll stay on board,' she replied without hesitation. The thought of a random sniper picking her out for target practice was terrifying. She shuddered. Kamal noticed and put his arm around her.

'Don't be afraid,' he whispered into her ears, 'I won't let anything happen to you.' Somehow the way he held her closely to his body and the strangely hypnotic amalgamation of a musky fragrance and his scent made her believe in him, that no harm would touch her. Was it possible to feel so incredibly safe in someone's arms, she wondered, resisting firmly the urge to put her head back on his shoulder and snuggle there.

Instead, she stood straight, aware of every nerve of her body tingling with the contact with his body. The security officer turned to her, his grim face lined by the years at sea. 'We will have security watching you at all times. In the unlikely event that an intervention is required, we will come in,' he said. 'But we don't think he will do anything risky. Plus he has no idea that we know, so that's an advantage.'

Rhea was told to play along and agree when John asked her to carry the parcel ashore. 'Say yes when he asks you to meet him in an isolated spot of the ship to collect the parcel. We will not be able to do this is the midst of a throng of passengers disembarking.' She agreed. With all the details of the plan chalked out, she and Kamal exited the conference room and went towards the deck, walking with no particular destination in mind. His arm, she noted, was still around her shoulder and she was reluctant to move it off.

'His people will cut me into little pieces and feed me to the fish,' she moaned. 'I have an ageing relative on board with a weak heart and a very loud voice. I am the only surviving child of ageing parents; I can't risk being killed on this trip.'

Kamal looked at her with an amused gaze and tilted her chin up towards him. 'Look at me,' he commanded.

Her eyes sought his out like magnets. Up close his eyes were two pools of honeyed caramel, fringed with thick dark lashes. It felt like he was looking right into her head.

'Stop being a wuss. And do what they tell you to. Surely they will keep your safety in mind.'

She shivered again. 'Are you feeling cold?' he asked, raising one eyebrow. 'Or is that the wuss in you again?'

She shrugged his arm off, miffed. 'I'm not being a wuss, Kamal Shahani! Don't you realize I could be killed?'

'Well, as they say, it is an adventure the moment you step out of your door. Look at it as an adventure, a story you could tell when you get back home about your close encounter with the drug cartel,' he winked. She melted.

'It's not you who could be killed,' she retorted, pouting.

'Well, you are the one who was making out with drug cartel members. You should have known these things could get dangerous.'

That hit low, below the belt. She drew a sharp breath and extricated herself from his arm. 'I didn't know,' she protested in a weak voice. 'How was I supposed to know? He seemed perfectly nice and respectable. They don't come with signs on their foreheads, do they?'

'You should have thought about that before you went into his room that night . . .' he whispered into her ear.

'Nothing happened that night,' she hissed back in an undertone, 'I mean it had started to, but we stopped.'

'You seem to be an expert at starting and stopping.'

Another blow. 'Damn you, Kamal. And why should I give you any explanation of what I did or didn't ?'

'Then don't.'

Rhea was annoyed. Why did she have to explain her choices to him and who she chose to make out with or not?

'We're here,' he said as they finally reached her cabin and put out his hand for the door card. She fished it out of her sling bag and handed it to him. He swiped the door open and gestured gallantly for her to enter.

'Thank you,' she said in a small voice, realizing that her heart was beating wildly and that she wanted him to bend down, gather her in his arms and crush her lips beneath his, despite the minor argument they had just had. They stood outside the door, faintly aware of Rina Maasi who was fast asleep. The static electricity between them could probably cause a small combustion if they touched, she thought.

'Thank you for helping me with this. You really didn't need to drop me back to the cabin.' She spoke in barely above a whisper, not wanting to wake up Rina Maasi and have to give a long-drawn explanation about why she was so late and being escorted back by Kamal.

'Just ensuring you reach safe and sound. You might just go back to the decks you shouldn't be on and overhear more dangerous stuff,' he said and turned to leave.

'Wait,' she said, suddenly not wanting the night to end and for him to go back to his cabin or wherever it was that Sonia was staying on the ship. He stopped still and turned around. His face was questioning and his eyes darkened when he saw the expression on her face. He took two steps towards her, put his arms on her waist and bent his head down towards hers. She reached her own arms up and wound them around his neck. His mouth descended upon hers and pressed her lips open with soft, fluttering kisses which then changed into a deep, exploratory kiss that left her breathless.

They broke away, breathing heavily, for just a moment, before he pulled her right back against his body. His hands ran over her and he groaned softly, nibbling at the nape of her neck as she arched herself into him. 'Not here . . .' he muttered. She realized the door to the cabin was still open. She pulled away.

'Goodnight,' she said, though every nerve in her body screamed otherwise. He closed his eyes, his breathing ragged, and then put a hand gently to her cheek and caressed it with his thumb. She was tempted to turn her head and kiss his fingers but knew that if she did, there would be no stopping them.

'Come with me.'

She looked up at him. He stared at her, his thumb still stroking her cheek.

'Goodnight,' she said, shaking her head.

He gave her a long, pleading look. 'Are you sure?'

'I am,' she replied, her voice still a whisper. 'Now I have to go in. Rina Maasi might wake up and wonder where I am.'

He angled his head towards the cabin where Rina Maasi's light snores could be heard. 'You would rather spend the night listening to that?'

She laughed and shook her head.

'Not really. But the option might get me into more trouble than I already am in right now.'

He gave her a long look and let go of her hand, dropping his arm from the wall, leaving her free to leave and break the connection between them.

She turned towards the door and stood there for a long, long moment, beating herself on the head with her imaginary club, and then turned around, telling herself that if he was still there, waiting, she would run and go back with him to his cabin to be done with this madness that was consuming her. He was already striding down the long passageway, without a backward glance. Despair washed over her, much like the sea water they were cutting through in this megalithic ocean liner. She entered the cabin as quietly as she could.

Rina Maasi stirred briefly under the covers. The dim light had been left on thankfully and she navigated herself to her bed.

'I hope you haven't been doing anything you shouldn't,' Rina Maasi said suddenly, her voice clear and loud in the silence, sitting upright like a Jack in the box. Rhea was startled. 'No Maasi, I haven't,' she said, feeling a bit guilty about not telling her that she was doing something even more dangerous.

'Kamal came around a couple of hours ago, asking for you,' Rina Maasi said primly. 'He wouldn't tell me why. And I heard his voice outside the door right now. Is there something I should know?'

Her breath caught at her throat. A couple of hours ago. That would have been barely minutes after she had seen Sonia and him at the elevator, and seconds after she had rushed off in shame and embarrassment at being caught watching them. Why did he come searching for her, she wondered. Strangely enough, they had exchanged kisses but not their phone numbers like it was in modern dating etiquette. But then, they weren't dating.

'It's okay,' she replied, 'I bumped into him on the deck during my walk, it was nothing important.'

Rina Maasi switched on the bedside lamp and sat up, looking at Rhea with the kind of eye that Medusa patented, to turn unwary onlookers into stone. 'It wouldn't have been "nothing important" if he took the trouble of coming here to chat with you. What is going on, child? I thought you were keeping a safe distance from him? I hope you realize that he comes from a completely different world. It's not a world we know or inhabit and are better off far away . . .' her voice trailed off.

'We've had this discussion before, Rina Maasi. You have nothing to worry about,' Rhea replied, feeling the resentment rise within her that her own aunt thought she wasn't good enough for Kamal.

'Anyway, goodnight child. You can't take away my right to worry about you, that's the one thing I'm really good at. Once it was an entire school of kids, but now I only have my nieces and nephews to be concerned about.'

Rhea smiled. Rina Maasi, like her mom, was a card carrying member of the Worry Club. The only difference was that her mom would talk endlessly about what could possibly go wrong and Rina Maasi would drop the occasional zinger right when you were lulled into somnambulism.

'Goodnight, Rina Maasi,' Rhea said. The cabin was dim and calming with the eerie glow of the night lamp which Rina Maasi insisted on having on for her nocturnal visits to the bathroom.

Soon soft, squishy snores began emanating from Rina Maasi's side of the cabin. Rhea's mind re-lived the kiss and all the moments of the day which were adding up slowly and steadily to completely confuse her, right up to the message from Samir on her phone. The one good thing about the cruise and all the other events that were happening in quick succession on it was that she hadn't thought of Samir in a long, long while. Not until his phone call in the evening. She closed her eyes and said his name but the wrench of pain that would inevitably stab her at the thought no longer came.

She tried again. 'Samir,' she said softly, under the blankets. All that came to mind was Kamal, standing in front of her, tucking her hair back behind her ear and off her face before leaning in to kiss her, making her knees become jelly in sixty seconds flat.

The next day was a day at sea. Rina Maasi was still resting her bones which continued to ache from the previous day's excursion. She was glad to spend her day in the cabin, emerging only briefly for lunch, and then demanding to be left on a sun bed in a shaded spot on the Promenade Deck, duly supplied with wine and Colonel Singh to keep her entertained.

'You wander around and do something,' she waved Rhea away. 'Don't babysit me. Go out, have fun.' Not that Rhea had any intention of doing so, but she didn't want to invite Maasi's wrath by saying so. Rina Maasi looked like a vivid bird with her copper head, big sunglasses and red lipstick, and dressed in a bright baroque patterned kaftan that entered the room before she did. She was not yet told about Samir's messages and it sat on Rhea's conscience like a preying vulture. She waved her aunt goodbye.

The pile of events in Rhea's life was getting higher and she felt the need to talk to Priya more than ever. She really needed to find a cyber café and chat with her best friend if she was online. She located a well-lit, cheery cyber café and went in.

With a sigh of delayed pleasure she surfed the net to catch up on how the world had decimated itself while she was busy trying to stop falling in love with an infuriatingly handsome man.

Priya wasn't online—not on Skype, not on Gchat, not even on Facebook—so she wrote her a long email, detailing all that had happened since she had left the desi shores. A little more surfing later she realized that in order for the plan to nail down the drug cartel to succeed, she could not remain cocooned in the inner recesses of cyber cafés but be in full technicolour visibility. After all, she had to make contact with John. As she emerged from the café, putting her wallet back into the little orange sling bag, she collided into someone who was turning the corner in a hurry.

'Whoa there, pretty lady!' John said in his familiar husky voice. 'You're just the person I wanted to see. Where have you been hiding?'

'Hello,' she said, trying to be polite and with her radar up on the mission.

'Haven't seen you around for the past few days.'

'I've been here and there,' she replied, being needlessly defensive. 'I've been around.'

And I overheard you last night. I know your evil plans, she was tempted to add.

'So what have you been up to since we last met? You ran off in a hurry,' he winked.

'I wasn't feeling too well that evening. But there's only so much one could be up to on a ship,' she replied, egging on his interest in her.

'Would you like to join me for coffee, or perhaps, a drink?' he asked, waving a generous hand in the direction of the deck which housed the bars and restaurants. Rhea snuck a glance at her watch, it was 11.30 a.m., not even legally afternoon. 'Okay, sure, why not?' she replied.

He led the way gallantly to the English-style pub on the deck which seemed to be already attracting the patrons. It had a dark panelled wooden interiors and a nautical theme with a mock anchor hanging menacingly on a wall right above them, making Rhea cast an occasional apprehensive eye at it every few seconds. This could be my Damocles sword, she thought to herself, it could fall down and knock her senseless. 'Would you like to move to another table?' he asked after her fifth glance up in as many minutes.

She looked around. The only other options were to perch at the bar, or sit in some ridiculously intimate tables meant for groping and toeing. 'No, I'm fine here. But if this decides to slip, I'll probably make it to the pearly gates quicker than scheduled.'

'You are the funniest little thing!' he laughed, sipping his ale in measured sips, like someone who knew how to make a mug of beer last because he didn't want to get drunk but had every intention of making the person he was with sloshed.

'I assure you it poses no concussion risk. And if you do get concussed, don't fear. I won't take you to my cabin and have my evil way with you.'

After some more conversation and flirting, he finally asked her if she could do him a favour and take a parcel into port the next day for a friend.

'I don't feel up to a shore excursion but I promised a friend I would pass it on. They are just some medicines for his aunt, she's apparently suffering from something terminal although I'm not sure what exactly her ailment is. I'm just playing courier boy . . . he will meet you right as you come ashore, before you get into the excursion bus, so you don't have to worry about missing him,' his voice trailed off and became a husky caress. He reached out and took her hand, stroking it gently. 'Would you do me this favour, please?'

Of course, she had no option but to agree, and he thanked her profusely, kissing her hand in a manner that went out of style with the knights in the medieval ages. He wanted to drop it off at her cabin, but she dissuaded him. It would do no good to have him show up at the cabin and give Rina Maasi something to inquire about. 'Not a good idea with my aunt around. You can hand it to me just before we go onshore and I could keep it in my handbag. It isn't very big, is it?'

'No, not at all, just a small . . .' he made an ambiguous size between his thumb and forefinger, '. . . package.

Thank you so much. I was really in a fix and I didn't want to waste my day going ashore, I would rather spend it on board.'

'Haven't you spent too many of your shore excursions on board?' she asked, the alcohol giving her courage she did not possess at regular times.

'It's no fun going anywhere on my own,' his voice cracked a bit. 'I miss my wife. I try not to go to the places we went together because it hurts.'

She looked at him, feeling the natural tap of sympathy begin its run through her system. But then, the natural vein of cynicism had reared itself and told her sternly that the dead wife was probably a lie spun to milk sympathy from unsuspecting bleeding hearts.

They decided to meet a little before disembarking time the morning they hit port, at a relatively secluded spot on the first deck near the service exits. She turned the corner and swiftly dialled Kamal's cabin from the first phone she could find. The Captain was also updated about the developments and the plan for the next morning. She wondered if she should source a bulletproof vest and say her last goodbyes to her family and friends. She could write out her will, leaving her book collection to her cousin Dolly who loved reading and had to be surgically separated from the book she was reading.

The rest of the day was spent wandering around the ship and indulging in a long, restful afternoon nap, given that it was one of those hot Mediterranean days that had evil hot winds blowing across from the Sahara which drilled holes through the skin.

The morning they docked, Rhea called for room service so that she could finish breakfast early and give herself about half an hour before the appointed time to meet John. A security officer led her to the spot and waited, concealed, at a distance behind her as she looked on. From her vantage point she had a clear view of the empty deck where she arranged to take the package from John. She was fifteen minutes before the scheduled time, she was to meet Rina Maasi at the queue to disembark in forty-five minutes.

The further she kept Rina Maasi away from the business, the better for her sanity, Rhea thought. 'How much trouble could she get into on a ship in the middle of the sea? I should have known,' she could almost hear Rina Maasi say in the middle of a family lunch, after two gin and tonics down the hatch. 'She was busy coochie-cooing with the mafia and almost getting both of us thrown into prison. Or shot. Or whatever it is that these countries do to drug runners.'

Dot at the appointed time, John wandered out from the shadows of the inner recesses of the ship and stood looking around uncertainly. His hair was damp on his head, his shirt was unbuttoned dangerously, his feet were clad in flip flops and he exuded, she noticed from a distance, a strange foreboding menace that had absolutely nothing to do with his size. Her heart did the sonic boom beat so loudly within her chest cavity that she was sure it was audible across the deck.

He bounded up to her as soon as he spotted her, and gave her a hug. 'Here it is, and thank you so much. My friend will contact you as you get off the bus at the plaza, I've told him what you look like so he'll spot you.' He dug out a small packet from his waist band and handed it across to her. She smiled a tight smile and looked at it, suddenly terrified, as if it were a venomous reptile.

She reached out a trembling hand, hesitant to take it, just as customs officials and the cruise security rushed out from all around, one knocking him to his feet and the other grabbing the parcel from his hand. She backed away quickly and moved into the shadows of the deck where he couldn't see her anymore.

Two sniffer dogs from what seemed to be the local law enforcement agency were also brought to the scene. They barked ferociously, enough to drive onlookers up the wall. She watched on as one of the officers took out a pen knife and made a sharp slit in the packet, checking the white powder inside, putting a daub on his tongue and nodding. He zip-locked it in another plastic bag and wrote something on it with a black marker. John was handcuffed and led away. As they took him off, he looked around wildly, his eyes, for one long moment, staring at her through the cloak of shadows she had withdrawn into. The entire operation had taken not more than ten minutes, and she was very much alive. She shivered and walked backwards into a person who was standing there in the shadows. Two firm hands reached out and held her steady. She could feel her entire body tremble with fear. She knew who those hands belonged to without turning around and so she stayed still, reluctant to move. 'You shouldn't be creeping up on unwary people in this way,' she said, aware that the slight physical contact had already set her nerves jangling with a curious anticipation. She should have known it would be Kamal, curious to see how the entire trap would unfold.

'He's gone. They've arrested his accomplice and one more crew member who was in charge of the cargo in the hold. You don't have to worry now.'

She put her head back, sort of leaning against him, and allowing herself just that moment of bodily contact. Feeling the warmth of his body on her bare neck, she asked, 'I don't have to worry then?'

'Nope, you don't.' Somehow, she already felt safer with him around.

'Thank you,' she said. 'Thank you for being here. I always seem to be thanking you.'

'I couldn't let you deal with this alone, could I?' he replied. She could feel the heat of his body through the thin cotton T-shirt she had on. Her hands began quivering. She broke bodily contact and turned around with a start to find her face a few inches away from his, noticing for the umpteenth time that his lips were smoother than they legally should be.

'But you need to be more careful. Please stop getting flattered by the attention any man pays you.'

She gasped.

He continued. 'Anyone with half a head on his shoulder could see that John was a con man of the first order and he almost succeeded in seducing you.'

Rhea winced at the remark. Perhaps he had a point. But she was not going to allow him the pleasure of knowing she had conceded to him. It came from growing up being the gangly, pimply, bespectacled, nerdy kid who was only befriended because she was the principal's daughter. She had an overwhelming urge to be accepted and she bent over backwards for anyone who showed her a little affection.

'I can take care of myself,' she said curtly, taking two steps back.

'Yes, I saw that the other day at the disco, with him all over you and you too drunk to push him away or to walk out on your own.'

'Kamal Shahani, thank you once again for all your help,' she spat out, suddenly infuriated by his assumption that he was in charge of her, 'I would be obliged if you didn't appoint yourself as my keeper anymore.'

They stared at each other for a long moment, neither willing to break eye contact first. Then a cool voice piped up in the immediate vicinity.

'So here you are, darling, I thought I spotted you coming this way.' It was Sonia. She emerged from the end of the passageway, dressed in hot pants and a cropped top which left her almost illegally flat abdomen appealingly bare. Her face was devoid of any obvious make-up except, perhaps, a touch of lip gloss and a hint of eyeliner on her hazel eyes. Rhea noticed a small beauty spot at a perfect location just above her upper lip. Fresh and glowing, Sonia could take anyone's breath away.

She acknowledged Rhea with a polite yet distant smile and tucked her arm into Kamal's, instantly making them a unit. 'Shall we go? Naina and the kids are waiting for you, time to go ashore!'

Giving her a loaded look, Kamal walked off. She however noticed with evil delight that he gently disengaged his arm from Sonia's. Naina rushed up to him, dragging a kid with each hand, and happily handed over Jay to his uncle.

Rhea hugged herself briefly, rocking on the balls of her feet and trying to arrange her thoughts into coherency. She went down to where Rina Maasi was waiting for her. 'What happened, Rhea?' Maasi asked. Rhea realized her face must have been pale and wan with the stress of the morning. But she couldn't tell her aunt about it. She had sworn Kamal to secrecy too.

'Nothing, I was walking around. I don't feel like going ashore,' she said, and fished out her mobile. It was time to distract her aunt. 'Samir called last night. And this is the message he sent when I didn't take his call.'

'Oho, why didn't you take his call? Don't tell me you were being stingy about international roaming charges when it was something so important.'

'I was just too shocked to talk to him at that moment. Honestly, Maasi, I didn't know what he was going to say and what would my response be.'

Maasi sat down on a convenient bench and put her reading glasses back on her nose from the chain it dangled on through the day. 'Ah,' she said, 'I can imagine, this must have really upset you.'

Rhea nodded meekly.

'Stay back on the ship if you don't feel like it. Think about it. What do you want to do? Sometimes it's best to let time settle things down. Do you still love him? Do you want him back?' she continued without waiting for an answer. 'What did you feel when you read the message, elation or fear?' This time she stopped, waited, and looked Rhea in the eye.

Rhea closed her eyes. 'I just felt panicky. Terrified. It didn't make me happy.'

'Then don't reply now. Let him suffer till you get back to Delhi. And then decide what to do.'

'Yes, you are right,' Rhea said hugging her aunt. She then turned around to go back to the cabin where she would draw the curtains and lie down, hoping to sort out this sudden sense of despair on realizing that she didn't love Samir anymore. Instead, she was falling head over heels for a man she had just met a couple of weeks ago.

TWELVE

After the last port of call, the passengers of Aqua Princess had a couple of days out at sea before their next halt at Cannes.

'So, have you decided what you're going to reply to Samir?' Rina Maasi asked the next morning at breakfast, just as Rhea was about to tuck into some sinful hashbrowns and sausages.

'I need more time, I can't decide.'

They ate their breakfast in silence. As they sipped their tea, Rina Maasi cast a narrowed look at Rhea. 'You have time till we get back, darling, enough time to come to a decision. But remember, with every day, time is running out and you need to get settled. I see how worried Shakun is, and you have your biological clock ticking away you know, tick tock, tick tock, can't stop it.'

Shakun, Rhea's mom and Rina Maasi's sister, had stopped a millimetre short of banging her head on the wall when Samir bailed out on the wedding. She assuaged the fury in her breast by spending ten minutes abusing him with the choicest expletives that no one could have imagined she possessed in her repertoire. After venting out her anger, she sheepishly confessed that she stole the words from Kareena Kapoor's character, Geet, in *Jab We Met*. 'And *sachi, dil thoda halka ho jaata hai*,' she had confessed to feeling lighter after that.

'A little rich for you to talk about biological clock and time running out Rina Maasi, when you filed for divorce within a few months of getting married.'

'My circumstances were very different from yours, Rhea,' Rina Maasi replied, looking a little upset. 'I was married against my wishes to a man who was much older than me and who repulsed me physically. When I got myself a job that ensured I wouldn't need to be dependent on my parents for either a place to live or financial support, I filed for divorce. That doesn't mean that I advocate staying unmarried.'

The morning sun streamed in through the window of the cabin and lit dizzying patterns on the floor and ceiling. 'But never mind me and my life. What are you doing here, shuttered inside the cabin when the entire ship is out and having fun? Go, enjoy yourself. Make some more friends, smile at people, go, go, go.'

Rhea trotted off dutifully to the poolside. Wearing a sundress over her turquoise bikini, she hoped against hope to bump into Kamal again. She was also carrying a large tube of sunblock. Just in case.

Strangely, the area was not crowded. Rhea assumed people had better things to do. She took off her sundress and moved into the pool, belly splatting the water surface in the shameful manner of the untrained. The water was warm thanks to the almost overhead rays of the sun and it felt good against her skin.

Rhea tried front crawl—a stroke she had not yet refined—and swam the length of the pool a couple of times, carefully avoiding the other swimmers who were in a more relaxed mode and floating around. After a few laps, she climbed out, dried herself with a towel and stretched out on the sun bed. It started getting hotter and the sun's rays almost reached the little awning where her bag was. Naina spotted her bag and grabbed the next deck chair, pretty in a floppy sunhat and a hibiscus flower print sarong over a bandeau bikini.

They greeted each other with an air kiss and a hug and got down to some girly conversation. Naina was in an unusually chatty mood. 'It feels good to have a conversation which doesn't have "Stop it now, don't touch that", every five minutes,' she confessed. The kids had been deposited in the play zone and would not emerge from that haven of jungle gyms, activities and storytelling sessions until lunch time.

'My brother, unfortunately, seems to have no time for me, now that Sonia's here,' she said laughing, completely oblivious to the sharp knife like effect that the words had on Rhea. 'I'm so bored all by myself these days and there's only so much under-age company I can deal with. I long for a meal where I don't have to spend all my time cutting food into bite sized portions on adjoining plates.'

Which explained, she thought, why she hadn't seen Kamal around. Rhea did a fake laugh. 'Of course, I'm much in the same boat. My aunt and the Colonel have me as the unwanted third leg and I would rather dine on my own than sit awkwardly while they play who blinks first. It does get a little trying.'

Naina continued, 'I hope they get together again. Sonia is trying her very best to bring him around, and she's a nice girl. Our families have known each other for years and we've practically grown up together.'

Rhea nodded politely at the use of the word 'nice' for Sonia but that debate was for another time. She pulled out her novel and opened it to the bookmarked page to try and get Naina to stop discussing Sonia and Kamal. Thankfully she took the hint and turned the conversation towards the hunky lifeguard who was now smiling in their direction. What's the use of being newly divorced if she couldn't flirt a bit with a complete stranger! After some time Rhea decided that she should apply her own sunblock since there seemed to be no volunteer in the immediate vicinity that morning. Naina downed her tall glass of fresh orange juice, plucked herself up from the chair and casting off her sarong, made her way through the scattered chairs to the pool, all the while keeping her eye on the muscled lifeguard. She dived into the water and then raised a lazy hand asking for his attention. He half-smiled and dived right in. Rhea choked back laughter as she watched on until she just got bored and decided to head back.

She gathered her things and began to walk towards the cabin to get dressed for lunch. Her mood had suddenly darkened and she realized that the sick, dull ache in the pit of her stomach was jealousy. 'Don't be silly, Rhea,' she told herself, 'You barely know the man; two kisses and one back rub does not mean a relationship. And there is Samir, waiting for you, apologizing . . . ah, well, you can get him to grovel when you get back. Don't be a fool over Kamal. He was probably just amusing himself with you.'

Nonetheless, she spent the rest of the day holed up in the cabin, sitting in the balcony, reading her book and avoiding all company.

The next morning dawned bright and blue, and busy because it was to be port day at Cannes. Rhea decided not to hide any longer and face the world, one which Kamal and Sonia were a part of.

The cruise liner anchored in the bay and they were tendered into the quay by smaller boats, passing the gorgeous yachts anchored along the way. The standard excursion plan they had signed up for included a tour of the Palais des Festivals at the Boulevard de la Croisette where the famous Cannes Film Festival takes place every year, a walk down the promenade and seeing handprints of stars at the Allee des stars which is the Cannes equivalent of the Hollywood walk of fame. They would then move into the old town before going onwards to Grasse to see how perfumes were made. Rhea's shore excursion group had the Colonel and his family, Naina and the kids, and a disgruntled looking Kamal with Sonia. She noted, with some jealousy, that Sonia was looking resplendent in a thin white linen shirt worn over tan shorts and a huge straw hat. Though she did not look at Kamal more than what was essential for a customary greeting, she was aware of his eyes on her almost all the time. The last time they had met, she had asked him to steer clear of her and as was apparent by the past few days, he was doing just that. Rhea hardly had any affinity towards perfumes—she used just the requisite amount for mandatory grooming—and therefore had no interest in visiting Grasse to see how it was made. What she wanted to visit instead was Saint Paul de Vence, a sixteenth-century village that was barely an hour away. 'It is the oldest medieval village in France. Marc Chagall is buried there and it's only an hour away from Cannes,' she hissed in a fierce undertone to Rina Maasi, trying to change her mind. But Rina Maasi, being her prosaic self, would not change plans and skip the excursion that she had paid for, for one that would need extra payment. That, and also the fact that it would require a lot of steep climbing, something that both she and the Colonel would be uncomfortable with.

'The last I saw you keen on any artwork was the join-by-dots painting books of your childhood. Believe me, one grave looks much the same as the other and we'll find you some graves to look at in Grasse. Every little town has graves. I can show you graves back in Simla too,' she said in a stentorian tone that brooked no argument.

Rina Maasi's voice, trained by long years of putting rioting classrooms of adolescent boys into order, had the entire bus load of cruisers looking at them curiously. Rhea was tempted to defy her and insist on going alone, but as always, she regressed to being a tongue-tied five-year-old. She felt her cheeks flame into glorious red from the embarrassment and her eyes began to tear up in frustration.

As they stumbled out onto the cobble-stoned streets of the old city, Rhea asked the tour guide if there was any way she could get into another tour to Saint Paul de Vence instead. 'You can take a taxi or drive,' he said, adding, 'But it will not be my responsibility. You have to be back in the ship by 5.30 p.m. It's 1 p.m. already. One hour to Saint Paul and one hour to drive back.'

Rhea fidgeted uncomfortably. She didn't have the courage to take a bus trip on her own, at least not without knowing the language of the country.

'I don't drive,' she almost whispered back, dejection sagging her shoulders. 'I mean I do, but I'm not confident enough to drive in another country.'

'Then you can rent a car with a driver,' Jean-Paul informed politely and dismissed her by turning his attention back to his scattered flock who had to be herded back into the bus from their wanderings around the stores.

'I can drive anywhere,' said a familiar voice behind her. She turned around with a start. It was Kamal, looking with the kind of mocking gaze that would have normally infuriated her, but it only made her stomach lurch. 'It's only a few kilometres away and would be criminal to miss for some silly perfumeries. I can take you there.'

'Wha . . .' she began, confused, and not comprehending what he had in mind.

'Kamal, you don't have to . . .' she tried again but he took her hand and pulled her and the guide aside. 'I am taking this lady off the excursion and we don't want our money back. I take the responsibility of getting her back to the ship on time.'

Rhea's jaw clunked to the ground with a thud. 'I can't let you do that,' she protested weakly. 'Your family is here and you would much rather be with them than with me.'

'That's where you are so mistaken, Rhea Khanna,' he replied enigmatically. 'I would much rather be with you than with anyone else, even though you told me to stop being your keeper. I never intended on being that anyway. Now, let's go tell your aunt that you are going to Saint Paul de Vence with me. I don't think she will have any objections.'

It seemed futile to argue or protest and she was amazed to see Rina Maasi most unperturbed about her niece wandering off into the French countryside with a strange man. But then, Kamal wasn't a strange man to Rina Maasi, she had probably seen him graduate from knee-length shorts to long pants and knew him much better than she did.

From the corner of her eye Rhea could see Sonia turning to look at them from a store window where she and Naina were. They came out and she said something to Naina who then walked across the street with a small frown splitting her forehead. Kamal spoke to her, gently.

'Rhea wants to see a sixteenth-century village about twenty kilometres away. I'm taking her there and will meet you directly on the ship in the evening.' It was a tone that brooked no discussion, no argument and no questions. Sonia had joined them by then but before either of them could respond, Kamal took Rhea's hand and moved with swift strides to the other end of the road, where he inquired about a self-drive car rental agency.

There was one issue however. 'I know I can drive there but I need help with directions . . . are you any good?' he asked, pulling out his phone and keying in the destination's name to find the area's map.

She shook her head apologetically.

'I think it would be better to hire a taxi. It would save us precious time. If we had the entire day I might have still risked the self-drive, but we have,' he checked his watch, 'Under four hours from now to get there and back.'

She hadn't done anything risky since the occasional bout of binge drinking with her buddies before Samir came into her life and sobered her up into blandness. He had been intent on moulding her into an image of himself—prim and proper, not a hair out of place, never mind her suspicion of his perfect hairline owing credit to hair plugs. Could she dare do something spontaneous? Could she dare go with the moment?

She looked at him, intent on his plan of getting them to their destination, and smiled. His eyes blazed into molten chocolate in response and his grip on her hand tightened.

'Are you sure you want to do this? Your . . .' she paused delicately, '. . . friend and Naina might not like the idea of being left behind on the excursion bus while you come away with me on this . . .' She waved her hand weakly to indicate the line of taxis waiting outside the rental agency for tourists to hire them.

'It doesn't matter, I'm doing what I want to do. I'm not keen on trudging through a tour of perfumeries with forty other people I have no interest in being with when I could be seeing a town I want to visit instead and spend time with you.'

Rhea gasped but he gave her no time to continue the conversation that gave her heart a flutter, and moved ahead to find them a taxi from amongst the line-up. She stood where she was, watching him have what seemed like a long and complicated discussion with a driver, involving a lot of shrugging and hand movements and rapid fire French. She was impressed that he spoke like a native, or at least well enough for a native to understand him. And voila! They found a driver who was willing to take them to St Paul de Vence and back and would throw in Antibes as well. All in good time!

'Have you agreed to pay a king's ransom for this?' Rhea whispered into Kamal's ear as they settled themselves in the taxi, acutely aware that sitting in the back seat of a taxi with someone so devastatingly handsome, and in such close proximity, was bad for her self-control.

'Yes,' he laughed back. 'But it will be so worth it.'

'I can't even begin to thank you enough . . .' she began, but he silenced her by putting a finger on her lips and taking her hand in his.

'Don't. Let's just enjoy the rest of the day.'

Rhea felt a warm feeling wash all over her. But the very next minute her body tingled with the awareness of each of his movements. Had it been a good idea to get away, alone with him? It was just for a few hours, how dangerous could it be, she rationalized, and hadn't she just been telling herself that she needed to be impetuous?

The taxi took them along the Mediterranean coast to the seaside town of Antibes, a resort destination for the rich and famous. They stopped briefly at the harbour to check out some of the world's biggest, sleekest and most expensive yachts at Billionaires' Quay. From there, they drove through the picturesque Provençal countryside with sunlight glinting hard off the green of the hills. The fortified village came upon them from the distance, high on a rocky spur in the countryside with its city wall ramparts standing out against the green of the hillside it was located on. The sight took her breath away.

'It's beautiful!' she exclaimed as the driver announced they were at St Paul de Vence. They checked in at the tourist office and got themselves a guide to take them through the village. As they walked through the narrow, cobbled walkways and arches, they realized that much of the village, with its stone walls, ramparts and archways, had remained the same since it was built centuries ago. The only discordant note, if any, were the throngs of tourists. That, however, did not deter their spirits as they visited art galleries in the medieval section of the town, climbing steep stone steps and lunching on a cheese sampler, goat cheese salad, lasagna, French onion soup and some rose wine. Rhea was careful to keep from gulping down the wine this time and sipped slowly to avoid getting into yet another episode of All Men Are Bastards that she had already played out with Kamal a couple of times before.

'So, all I know about you is that your fiancé ditched you,' he said over lunch. 'And that Soni ma'am is your aunt. Tell me more about yourself.'

'There's nothing to tell really. I did my post graduation in English honours, did a media course and landed a job in a publishing house as a copy editor which was hours upon hours of bone numbing copy checking work on technical manuscripts. I quit a few months before the wedding because I thought I would need time to set up my home and then get back to a regular job. In that period I took up some freelance assignments to keep body and soul together.'

She smiled at the memory of those days of worrying about not being able to pay the rent since she moved out of her parent's on a whim after her father started grumbling about her late working hours.

'And then, of course, my fiancé ran away to Bali with another woman on the honeymoon I was supposed to go on with him. So here I am, broke and heartbroken . . .'

'Are you really heartbroken?' he asked looking deep into her eyes, with an expression she could not fathom.

'Why would you say that?'

'Your body does not respond like that of one who is heartbroken,' he replied without breaking eye contact. Her cheeks flamed again, and she looked down at her plate, embarrassed.

'Let's not go that way,' she pleaded. 'I told you we should not, this is crazy and . . .'

'But whatever is crazy is always so worth it,' he replied, taking her hand again and making slow circles on the inside of her wrist.

She pulled her hand away. 'This isn't going to work, Kamal,' she said ruefully.

His face shuttered down as he replied, 'You aren't letting it work.'

She looked away and they ate the rest of their meal in a silence that was strained by words they did not dare to utter, words that would have shaken the fragile equilibrium of them being together in a place without sparring.

'Tell me about your work,' she ventured. He promptly launched into a detailed description of the start-up he founded with a couple of friends which began with online hotel reservations and had now ventured into food on demand through restaurant aggregation across the country. 'So now, if you are driving through a place, you could check the nearest restaurant on your route, place your order and pick up the parcel as you drive through, or opt to have it delivered to you if you are taking the bypass route around the town. All the restaurants we feature on our app are vetted to our standards of hygiene and quality by our own restaurant reviewers who have personally been there.'

'It seems like a fabulous idea,' she said, feeling proud of the man she had fallen for.

After lunch, they did the Marc Chagall tour. The twenty years he lived there resulted in a series of vivid paintings which were all about love. 'Which is why St Paul de Vence is a good place for lovers like you to visit,' their gentle guide said with a twinkle in his eye.' Kamal did not correct him and Rhea found herself rolling the thought in her head, over and over again. 'Lovers like you.' At the end they went to the Saint Paul de Vence cemetery. It was a simple white tomb, bare except for a blaze of wildflowers someone had placed on it.

'Good grief, it's almost 4.30 p.m.!' Kamal suddenly said looking at his watch and they sauntered down towards where their taxi was parked.

'We should make it back in time,' Rhea said hopefully, 'It took us less than an hour to reach, remember?'

As they sat in the taxi, the weather which had been so wonderful and bright all through the day, suddenly darkened into sulky and stormy angriness. A cutting wind began whipping through the road and with a wall of heavy rain the visibility dropped to barely a few feet ahead. The traffic dropped to a crawl as the road became a blur. All of a sudden, the car sputtered to a stop. The driver swore, begged her pardon for using intemperate language not suited for delicate ears, and then continued swearing merrily. He got out of the car, put the hood up and started tinkering around with the insides.

'Won't start,' he informed them through the storm. 'I'm calling for it to be towed to a garage. We have to find you alternate transportation.'

The hands on her wrist watch showed it was 5 p.m. She pulled out her phone to call Rina Maasi about the delay and saw a dozen missed calls from her. Some hand of God had put her phone into silent mode which is why she didn't hear her phone ring. In addition to the missed calls, there was also a spate of increasingly annoyed messages from her aunt. Rhea was sure Rina Maasi had fire and smoke coming out of her nostrils.

She took a deep breath, dialled her aunt's number. It was answered on the first ring.

'Where have you been, Rhea?' Rina Maasi yelled, making no attempt to mask either her anger or her relief. She was sure anyone standing in the immediately vicinity would have had their eardrums ruptured. 'Why aren't you here yet? We're already on the ship!'

'We've just left and have a slight problem with our taxi. But we should be there soon. Hold the boat for us,' she said, trying to sound chipper than she felt.

'Make it snappy, I'll let them know you are on your way.'

Rhea looked at her watch. 5.15 p.m. Her heart sank. Her stomach went fluttery and her palms went cold and clammy.

'Isn't there any way he can get this fixed?' Rhea asked Kamal, noticing his jaw getting tighter and grimmer and his discussion with Julien in the native tongue getting more and more clipped as he went out with him and fiddled a bit under the hood.

'Looks like this taxi is not going to get going until we get a mechanic here or take it to a garage. And we just have a quarter of an hour.'

The dark shadows of the surrounding made the entire scene rather ominous. Rhea almost burst into tears thinking that this was the result of sashaying off with another woman's man and defying the authority of her good aunt. Now she would be left in the French Riviera with not even a toothbrush or a change of undergarments and dangerously low funds on her already maxed out debit cards. A strangled half sob escaped her.

'Are we going to make it back in time?' She felt her face crumple with panic.

Kamal stared down at her, a perplexed smile creasing his face as he leaned back through the window of the taxi. 'I didn't think you would get scared so easily, Rhea. Don't worry, I'm going to get us back to the ship, in time and safe and sound. But probably not dry.' She laughed seeing his hair plastered to his head. No hair plugs here, she noted. His thin linen shirt was wet and clinging to his broad shoulders and chest and despite the situation they were in, Rhea reached out a tentative hand to touch it, feeling the searing heat of his body through the wet fabric. It was all the permission he needed. He pulled her to him and kissed her gently, not bothered that he was getting her soaked through her T-shirt. His hand reached out and cupped her breast, a thumb lazily caressing her nipple before pulling away and breaking the kiss abruptly, but gently, as she leaned into him for more.

'Don't stop,' she whispered.

'As much as I would like to continue, we need to find an alternate way back to the quay without getting left behind,' he said softly, pulling away and opening the door. Taking her hand, he pulled her out of the dry interiors of the taxi to the furious pelting rain outside where the driver was doing his best to hail down every passing vehicle that roared past, unheeding.

Within two seconds of stepping out, Rhea was drenched to the bone and felt the beginning of a shivering chill.

'Our only option is to take a lift or get an alternative taxi, which . . .' he looked up and down the almost deserted road, '. . . seems highly unlikely.'

The shiver going through Rhea's body was now more from fear than the chill. Kamal understood, and, drew her briefly towards him, giving her a brief, comforting hug. As they continued to wait in the rain, a pair of headlights closed in on them and stopped after their frantic waving. A quick conversation ensued between Kamal and the taxi driver of what turned out to be a van with some indeterminate cargo. Kamal paid the taxi driver and after some back slapping bonhomie, they clambered into the front of the tiny van. The driver, apparently lured by the promise of more than twice the amount of money he would normally make for a regular trip up and down the route, took on himself to drive at F1 lap speed to the pier. Rhea stuck to Kamal all along, his comforting arm around her.

Finally they reached, rattled, white and shaken, and scampered to the pier where they had a speed boat waiting to get them across to their ship. A frazzled crewmember who was holding their names on a placard breathed a sigh of relief. They made it just about five minutes before the 30 minutes extra allotted for late arrivals.

'Just made it,' Kamal said as he helped Rhea into the boat, the storm having strangely dissipated and the Cannes skies being once again clear and turning gloriously orange by a brilliant Mediterranean sunset. 'By the skin of our teeth,' she responded and they both smiled. He was gorgeous, she thought, and savoured the memory of the kiss in the taxi. The pounding rain, it seemed, was like a wall, keeping out the rest of the world. But now they had breached that wall and were back. Not that Rhea regretted it. The alternative of getting left behind was scary. They would have had to find a way to meet the ship at its next port of call. And more scarily, it would have involved spending more time alone with Kamal Shahani, risking her hormones to take over her sensibility.

On the boat, Kamal held her hand like it was the most natural thing on earth for him to do, and she letting it rest in his, like it was meant to be there, never mind the hazel eyed, alabaster skinned Sonia waiting for him on deck of the Aqua Princess.

'And so, the day comes to an end,' he said softly, looking into the distance where their liner awaited them.

'Thank you,' Rhea began, her voice strangely husky, wondering if their together moments were truly over. 'You were very kind to take me to Saint Paul's . . .'

Her voice caught some more on the jagged edge of some emotion that she couldn't place her finger on. 'God, I'm always either thanking you or apologizing to you. Why am I always misjudging you?'

He looked down at her, his expression tender, unfathomable. 'I misjudged you too, Rhea. We have both misjudged each other. You aren't what I thought you were . . . you are very different from most of the women I know.'

She looked out at the sea, hoping he wouldn't be able to see the tears pricking her eyeballs. A lump began to form in her throat which would definitely impede further conversation, so she was thankful of the choppy waters that put a stop to it. Nevertheless, it made her regret the overindulgence at lunch.

As they hopped on to the mothership, Rina Maasi, who was waiting, perched precariously over the railing, hurtled her way to them and hugged Rhea.

'I expected better from you, Kamal,' Rina Maasi began in a tone which had been sharpened to perfection over years of sharp speaking to errant adolescents. 'We were so worried, I'm sure my blood pressure has shot to the skies, what if both of you had been left behind?'

'Soni ma'am, you didn't need to worry, I would have ensured Rhea reached you safe and sound, no matter what.'

'It's a good thing Rhea's father isn't here, or he would have asked you about your intentions towards his daughter, and to declare them honourable.'

'Don't be ridiculous Rina Maasi. It was very kind of Kamal to volunteer to take me. And he made sure that I returned safely despite the storm and the broken-down taxi. You should be thankful.'

Rina Maasi fixed them both a stern eye. 'I will. And I am grateful. But, my dear, his motive wasn't all that altruistic as you make it out to be.'

Kamal grinned naughtily but from the corner of her eye Rhea saw Sonia stare at them. Her face was grim, her eyes cold.

THIRTEEN

The cruise was almost over. The next morning they would dock at port, stand in line, get their papers stamped, and disembark, travelling to Rome, the city they had arrived in, in what seemed now a lifetime ago, where a hotel awaited them and a couple of days later, a flight back to Delhi. Rhea's eyes opened with the rays of the morning sun streaming in through the porthole. She was surprised to see Rhea Maasi already up and sipping tea.

'Good morning, Rhea,' she said as she noticed movement beneath the covers and a still sleepy Rhea sitting up and rubbing her eyes.

'Good morning, Rina Maasi,' she mumbled before fleeing into relative privacy. Spending weeks with another person in a confined space was restricting, she realized, especially after getting used to her own little studio apartment.

She splashed some water on her face, brushed her teeth and looked at her reflection in the mirror. Why did Kamal kiss her the way he did? It was like a jigsaw puzzle but the trip to Saint Paul de Vence, the kiss, and all the tenderness didn't quite fit with the piece about the ex-girlfriend who had joined them midway. She examined herself and saw what she saw every day—an average looking face, a tall, lean torso, lesser cleavage than what she would have liked, and a stubborn jaw. What a stranger would have seen was a tall, leggy, lissome girl with golden skin, beautiful hair, and with the keen gaze of someone with more questions than she had the answers to. But having been brought up by parents who didn't believe in paying compliments, Rhea found it difficult to see herself as beautiful. People around her assumed her introversion to be snobbishness, and refrained from complimenting her.

Breakfast was a dreary affair, with a sudden pall of gloom seeming to have descended on the ship. Email addresses, phone numbers and other contact details were exchanged by those who wanted to stay in touch when back in their native lands.

Kamal was not to be seen anywhere and Rhea did not dare call him on his cabin phone. 'If he wants me, he knows where I am,' she told herself. It was unseemly to chase a man, she thought, and yet she wandered around the decks in hope of bumping into him. Still not spotting him anywhere, she wondered if he might have called her at the cabin. They still hadn't exchanged phone numbers. He knew her cabin number and could contact her if he wanted to. In a bid to distract herself, she pulled out her phone and went through the photographs they clicked during their trip to St Paul de Vence. She stopped at the one a store owner took of them together. The way they stood exuded a comfort which belied the fact that they hardly knew each other. We look like we belong together, Rhea thought. He was smiling and open faced with his arm on her shoulder while she had her head tilted into his chest.

'We should probably start getting packed,' Rina Maasi said coming out of the bathroom. They were back in their cabin and what Rina Maasi meant was that Rhea should start packing while she guided and supervised the process from her vantage point in the armchair. They were now rapidly headed back to Rome where the cruise terminated.

Packing was an exhausting affair. The luggage had to be kept outside the door at night with the appropriate colour coded tags on them, and only an overnight bag with what they would require the next morning was to be left with them. The entire process required proper planning and impeccable execution. Rhea would do the first round, then Rina Maasi would insist that she could do it better and create disorder out of order. Then, when the suitcases wouldn't zip even after being sat upon, the whole lot would need to be packed again, and this round would be done by Rhea who was rather OCD about ensuring that every available space was optimally utilized. And there was the ceramic ware which, she had a sinking feeling, was going to be part of their hand luggage, more specifically, hers.

'I wonder where Singhie is,' Rina Maasi said, referring to Colonel Singh who she had started calling by that name. Right on cue there was a buzz at the door. It was Singhie, in the flesh!

'There's Casablanca on in the movie theatre. Special show for us geriatrics. Would you care to join me?' he asked Rina Maasi who agreed promptly and tucked her arm into his, instructing Rhea to get the bulk of the packing done in the interim.

Rhea sighed and nodded. She began packing her own clothes first, and then Rina Maasi's. Lying on the dressing table, inconspicuous, she noticed a little box, a red velvet one, the kind they keep jewellery in. She opened it. Nestled within was the ring with the coral cameo, the one she had admired and tried on while shopping at Taormina. Crafted with exquisite Victorian filigree work around the edge, the ring was an antique as claimed by the store owner, and a little card within the box held proof of its antique value. She gasped in surprise and put it in her finger and admired it. It was a perfect fit! It had been when she tried it. How thoughtful of Rina Maasi! She must have noticed her trying it on and keeping it back with a pang of regret because of its price. She kept it on, admiring its design and the two diamonds set at either end of the oval, the grave expression on the face of the Victorian woman carved in semi-profile on it, her hair a mess of carefully arranged tendrils fluttering around her face.

She got back to her packing and finished putting all her stuff in and a fair amount of Rina Maasi's except a few odd items that they would still require. She then remembered about the farewell dinner on board and dug down into the carefully packed suitcase to pull out a navy sheath dress with a drop décolletage. It was a short number and therefore accentuated her long legs.

Her to-do list checked, Rhea decided to go the sundeck with a book. She wanted open space and fresh air to clear her head of all the confusion that kisses from a man she barely knew and SMSs from the man she almost married had created.

Finding a deserted spot, she settled back for a long, undisturbed read, only to realize that a shadow had fallen across her. She looked up, squinting against the sun and was surprised to see Sonia. She was probably bathed in an overbearing musky perfume, enough to asphyxiate anyone in two foot radius.

'Hello Sonia!' she said, uncertain as to why she was there.

'Hello,' came a cold reply. Nah, they couldn't bond over stories of boyfriends, bad hair cuts and wardrobe malfunctions. 'May I join you for a moment?' she asked more as a statement than a request and pulled the adjoining deck chair. She put her sunglasses up on her forehead in an All the Better to See You with My Dear manner, and ran her beautiful but ice cold eyes up and down Rhea. 'Yes?' Rhea said in her politest tone.

'It's about Kamal. You must have guessed so, what else would I have to discuss with you?'

Rhea held her peace and kept her expression bravely neutral. Sonia began. It was clearly a speech she had rehearsed. 'Kamal and I know each other since we were kids. Our families have known each other for a long time and we literally grew up together; it was expected that we would eventually get married to each other.' She paused and drew a deep breath. Rhea looked down at the cameo ring on her finger and twirled it around for lack of anything to say or do.

'Of course, he went abroad and came back, but we stayed in touch. We dated for a while and I expected him to pop the question anytime, but then there was a horrible misunderstanding. I can't really tell you the details but suffice to say that he left and I didn't get a chance to clarify my position to him. Which is why I am here.'

Rhea maintained a dignified silence, wondering if Sonia sparkled in direct sunlight. But Kamal was so handsome and tender and considerate and gentle and everything that Sonia didn't deserve, she thought. Or was it she who was to be blamed, coming into his life barely a couple of weeks back and expecting him to drop everything for her? After all, she barely knew anything about him except that he was a wonderful kisser, could speak fluent French and most importantly, was always around to get her out of trouble.

'So, what I am trying to tell you is, don't take the attention he's been paying you too seriously. He is just trying to get me jealous. Tomorrow we leave the ship and will go our different ways. And he will be back with me. Girls like you are nothing to him, he will use you, leave you and come right back to me. He has done it before and he'll do it again. I know him. He loves me.'

Sonia leaned forward towards her, her eyes glinting hard like two pieces of cold stones. Rhea noted with concern that her incisors seemed unnaturally sharp and backed away, putting a wary hand to her neck.

'I'm going to say it once more you little upstart and I'm going to say it loud and clear,' Sonia said, coming to the nub of the entire speech. 'Stop chasing Kamal if you know what is good for you, or you'll pay for it and so will that doddering old aunt of yours.'

The gloves were off. Rhea reeled a bit from her words but refused to give her the pleasure of a reaction. She stood up, gathered her book, and picked up her bag. 'Perhaps,' she replied, her tone doing the cold and cutting equally well, 'You should be using this time and effort to woo Kamal back because believe me, I am not the one doing the chasing.'

Sonia stood up, looked at a point behind Rhea's shoulder and stomped off. Rhea turned around in surprise to see Kamal standing there.

He had been listening to their conversation all the while but hadn't bothered to stop Sonia and her ranting. White hot rage poured through Rhea's veins and went straight to her brain. 'Rhea,' he put a hand out as though to stop her from moving, 'I can explain everything.'

'I don't want to hear your explanations, Kamal,' she said, choking back the sobs that had begun to rise up in her throat. 'This outburst by your ex-girlfriend was absolutely humiliating. Now please let me go.'

'Give me a minute,' he said, his voice pleading, and coming forward to block her way to the elevators. She side stepped him and strode off without a backward glance, her entire body shaking with rage.

She stomped into the cabin and threw herself on the bed for a good long sob. After around ten minutes of unrestrained crying, she paced around the cabin, kicking a dustbin here, a side table there, until Rina Maasi came back from what seemed to be a tiring day on board.

'What's the matter?'

'Nothing,' she replied, directing another angry kick at an offending footstool.

'Is it something to do with Kamal?' Rina Maasi could be accused of many things but not being perceptive would not be on that list.

'Yes. I got told by La Plastica to keep away from him,' Rhea replied, 'I told her to tell him to keep away from me because it's him trying to get into my pants and not vice versa.'

'Your language is execrable but I get your point and your angst.'

'I'm not in a good mood.'

'So perhaps it's a good thing we finish the cruise tomorrow and then both of you can go your separate paths,' she said.

A flash of disappointment crossed Rhea's face swiftly, but it didn't miss her aunt's eye. 'Dear girl, don't tell me you've fallen in love with him?'

She received no coherent response other than a vague sound.

'I understand how easy it is to fall for that boy. Half the population of the adjoining girls' school would climb up the wall to catch a glimpse of him in the march-past.'

Rhea stared morosely out of the porthole, wondering if she had fallen in love with Kamal, or if what she was experiencing was that totally unreliable thing called an infatuation which was bound to fade on familiarity.

'I don't know what it is, Rina Maasi,' she began to sob. 'It's just that I can't get him out of my head. I sound and feel like a sappy, love struck adolescent and it's really disturbing because barely three weeks ago I thought I was in love with Samir and was ready to marry him. Tell me, am I being silly? Will I get over this once I'm back home and back to the routine?'

Rina Maasi hugged her and sighed deeply. 'You are being silly and you will forget all about him once you get back home and we begin setting you up with eligible boys. That is if you don't plan on getting back with Samir.'

The horror of being paraded before prospective grooms by her worried mother, grim father and tittering cousins dawned on Rhea's mind, clear as crystal.

'Oh no!' Her jaw dropped.

'Oh yes,' Rina Maasi countered. 'Be practical. You're almost thirty. Your eggs will start withering up and dying. Once you're back I'm sure your mother will have lined up a slew of prospective grooms for you, and you'll have to choose one because they will want to marry you off as soon as possible.'

Rina Maasi looked at the growing consternation on Rhea's face and burst into peals of echoing laughter. 'I'm kidding, child. Just be careful, it's easy to fall for someone you barely know from a two-week vacation in which you were thrown together constantly. But how you are when you get back to the regular routine is what really matters. Will this continue, or will you both get back to your routine lives and move on?'

She came up to Rhea and held her in a tight hug, surrounding her with the comforting fragrance of faded perfume that made Rhea bawl her eyes out all over again and almost burst a vein in her nose with all that honking.

'Gosh, you are being snot-nosed on my silk blouse,' Maasi said. 'I don't think you sobbed half as much when your fiancé ditched you at the last minute to run off with that chest.'

Rhea nodded. It was true. She had taken Samir's betrayal squarely on with a determined chin and got down to the practicalities of cancelling everything, getting refunds, and returning whatever could be returned to the stores. What was not taken back, Rhea made the effort of hawking them online.

Was she making up for the lack of a burst of emotion now? Suddenly Rhea wasn't sure if she was crying for Kamal or Samir, or both of them.

Rina Maasi lay down on her bed and dozed off into a deep nap, punctuated by an occasional snore. There was the formal dinner to look forward to but Rhea was in no mood to go for it. She sat still in one place, thinking about her life till Maasi woke up from her afternoon siesta. Then she prepared tea for both of them.

'I hope you're not planning to stay in for the farewell dinner?'

She nodded.

She had been planning to lock herself in the cabin and call in for food but Rina Maasi would have none of it.

'Don't be silly, you have to come to dinner. Why should you cloister yourself just because an insecure woman is worried her boyfriend is making a play for you?' She patted her arm gently. 'Now please go soak your eyes and rid them of that redness. I won't do to have my niece sobbing all through the last formal dinner on board, looking like a red-eyed rabbit.'

Rhea laughed and hugged her aunt, noticing that she looked frailer despite the fact that she had just woken up from her siesta. It could be all the exertion of being on the cruise. She made a mental note of insisting she got a complete health check-up when they landed back in India.

They dressed up to the nines and Rhea even managed to convince Rina Maasi to ditch the bright red lipstick in favour of a pale pink. While they debated about what jewellery to wear and unlocked the safe in the room to take out their valuables, Rhea realized she hadn't thanked her aunt for the ring she had been flashing on her finger.

'By the way, thanks for the ring, Maasi,' Rhea said.

'Which ring?'

Rhea displayed her adorned finger.

'Oh, isn't this the same ring you tried on when we went ashore in Sicily? I didn't get you that, where did you find it?'

Rhea was taken aback. 'The box was on my bedside table.'

'I didn't get it,' Maasi said again.

'How did it get here then?'

'I have absolutely no clue. Ask the room steward, he might know.'

'I will,' she replied and resolved to do so the moment she came across the ever-smiling young man who was in charge of their cabin.

Leaving the conversation at that, they dressed up and walked to the main dining hall where the party was. The Captain was at the entrance along with the cruise director, welcoming everyone. He shook Rhea's hand for a long time and thanked her for helping them.

'What was that about?' Rina Maasi asked, confused.

'Oh nothing, look there's your Colonel,' she changed the topic effectively. The Colonel was waiting for them at the entrance with his family and they all went to the table they had got specially assigned for themselves.

Before the waiters could begin service, the Colonel stood up, looking rather dapper in a three piece suit, and tinkled a glass to get everyone's attention. The table fell silent.

'I have an announcement to make,' he said, smiling fondly at Rina Maasi who went coy and simpering in two seconds flat.

'I have asked Mrs Soni to marry me and she has very kindly accepted. We will be married two months from now, back in India.' Rina Maasi put up her left hand, which was now newly adorned with a delicate ring with five tiny diamonds in a brilliant starburst. Rhea gasped, she had no idea! So caught up in her own life, she failed to notice Rina Maasi's new piece of jewellery, one that was so symbolic.

Congratulatory wishes filled the air. The Colonel's son and daughter-in-law hugged him and then Maasi in joy.

'You didn't mention a thing, Rina Maasi!' Rhea burst out heatedly. 'This is such a surprise.' After the initial shock and anger of being kept in the dark, a wave of happiness came over her for her aunt. She hugged her tight, tears of joy running down her cheeks. Finally Rina Maasi had found her companion, she would not be alone in her old age, Rhea smiled at the thought.

'Well, I have been wearing it for over a day, you were just too caught up to notice,' Rina Maasi whispered into her ears as she hugged her back. 'It came as quite a surprise to me too. But I was not going to let a good man pass me by. I suggest you don't too.'

And with that cryptic comment she allowed herself to be swept away into the circle of her newly acquired family, complete with children and grandchildren, hugging and cheering.

Champagne was popped and Rhea allowed herself more of the sparkling drink than she could handle. The world around her began to spin, whether it was the sudden acceleration of the liner or the champagne, she didn't know. Kamal, Sonia and Naina were at their regular table at the other end of the dining hall, and Rhea studiously avoided looking in that direction although she could feel Kamal's eyes on her like two needles. Rina Maasi returned to her chair and sat down heavily, her breath suddenly strained and her face ashen. She picked up her napkin and placed it on her lap, when, without warning, her face turned a sickly white. Before Rhea could inquire what was wrong, she slid down to the floor.

FOURTEEN

The rest of that night was the kind of nightmare that one imagines could happen only to other people, in other stories. Rhea could only remember the events of the night in kaleidoscopic flashes. Rina Maasi lying on the floor, her face pale, her breathing ragged. The sudden flutter of conversation stopping and intensifying as everyone craned their necks from their tables to see what had happened. A passenger, also dining in the same dining hall, rushing across, announcing he was a doctor and beginning to check Maasi's vitals. The Colonel kneeling by her side and holding her hand which was as limp as a baby bird's broken wing. Everything in slow motion.

A stretcher was rushed in, accompanied by the ship's doctor who was in an evening jacket but had a stethoscope hanging around his neck. She was taken to the sick bay with a retinue of attendants that included Colonel Singh, his family, Rhea and surprisingly, Kamal.

He had been three tables away with Naina when Rina Maasi had fainted and was at her side before Rhea could react. He had indicated to the crew that it seemed like an emergency and got the paramedics up to the restaurant, helping with transferring her to the stretcher.

In all the confusion that got Rhea panicking, he took complete charge of the situation. 'Does she need to be airlifted to a hospital? Which is the closest port? Do we need to call in a helicopter?' he threw around the questions in a way that made Rhea grateful for having someone around with a calm head in a tense environment.

A nervous Rhea didn't know whether Rina Maasi's medical and travel insurance took care of hospitalization and sundry charges. A helicopter, she guessed, wouldn't come cheap. Just as she thought of calling up her father, things began to improve and Rina Maasi came around. She was groggy but a stroke was thankfully ruled out.

'Her blood pressure seems normal now. It doesn't seem like anything serious. She had probably been over exerting herself all day and not watching what she's been eating,' Dr Mulroney, a kind-eyed gentleman, said. With his steel grey mop of hair done in a crew cut and sharp manners, he seemed more like a general in the army.

'Air-lifting not required at all,' he said, responding to Kamal's query. 'All her vitals are now stable. I'm just keeping her in as a precautionary measure, given her medical history. Hopefully, she should be back to normal with a little rest. But I'm not taking the risk of sending her back to her cabin without running some more tests. She should be fine enough to disembark and travel.'

Given that they were to disembark the very next day, it seemed like a scary proposition to Rhea. Once they were off the ship and headed their separate ways, how would she manage if anything like this were to recur on their long journey back home? But then, there was the Colonel who was now morally duty bound to pitch in and take responsibility for Maasi, she thought. Perhaps they could change flights to travel together. Sitting next to Rina Maasi who was hooked up on various machines that kept beeping incessantly, the Colonel looked at her with tender concern. His devotion to his new fiancé was palpable and Rhea's face softened as she watched him. She, however, avoided looking at Kamal. Everytime she did, Sonia's words kept replaying in her head, making her blood boil.

Rina Maasi stirred and promptly started grumbling about how cold it was, and why was she lying down in her saree, and God, wasn't there anyone who could have taken out the pins in her hair before putting her head on the pillow?

'I'm sure one of those damn hair pins has punctured my cranium.'

'Language, Maasi, language,' Rhea laughed, knowing that her aunt was now surely on the Bend.

She went up to her to remove the offending hair pin, and also any other pins with potential to hurt. Rina Maasi was changed into a medical gown and her clothes and jewellery were handed across to Rhea to deposit back into the room. It was the early hours of the morning and Rhea swayed on her feet from hunger and tiredness. The Colonel had retired to his room. Taking a seat next to Rina

Maasi, Rhea held her hand, feeling the reassuring warmth of her fingers clenching hers. She realized that her aunt may behave like a battle axe but she was the only kindred soul Rhea had in the family. The only one who had always indulged her, stood up for her, especially when everyone insisted that it must have been something she had done to turn a worthy man away.

'Go sleep, you look terrible,' Rina Maasi told her, completely unaware that had she seen a mirror, her own reflection would terrify her.

'All I need is some rest. I am exhausted by the travel, that's all. Go eat first and then sleep. You've had a long night,' she instructed Rhea in the tone of one who isn't used to her diktat being defied. 'The poor thing must be starving,' she mumbled aside to Kamal, who was standing close by, trying hard to be unobtrusive. 'Go feed her something. I can't have her fainting too. As it is, she's underweight.'

'I'm not underweight, I'm fine. I just have a high metabolism and a lean structure,' Rhea said, a little angry for having to defend her metabolic rate in front of a man who now probably thought she stuck fingers down her throat after every meal. But she had to concede that her stomach was empty and growling. It had been a while since her last meal.

'Nonsense!' said Rina Maasi. 'You don't eat at all. Maggi, biscuits, sandwiches, bah, that's not food. I can't remember the last time I saw you eating healthy. When you get to my age, you'll have your bones turn to chalk and snapping into two at every movement.'

'I'm not going anywhere and I'm not hungry,' Rhea repeated, ignoring Rina Maasi's little lecture on her appalling eating habits and putting on a determined expression that usually scared off most men who found her attractive. 'I'm waiting right here till you're okay.' And she had every intention of doing so despite the fact that there seemed to be no footstool to rest her aching feet that her stilettos from the previous night's party were killing slowly. 'Don't worry,' said the medical assistant who was now checking the drip Rina Maasi was hooked up to, 'We'll be here to keep a watch on her. Anyway, she's falling asleep now and will not wake up until after a few hours. The doctor's orders are that she will be kept under observation till morning, so you might as well go grab something to eat and get some sleep. You can come back later.'

Sure enough, Rina Maasi started snoring gently, her flame red hair standing out brightly against the white pillow case, contrasting even more with the pallor of her skin, and her nostrils flaring out slightly with each breath. Rhea realized how frail and vulnerable she looked, far from the dragon she pretended to be when she was awake.

She stood up uncertainly. Kamal moved quietly to accompany her out into the passageway towards the elevator bank. 'I could do with a bite myself. We could grab something to eat at one of the 24-hour cafés. I suspect the restaurants would be shut,' he suggested. A capsule elevator arrived and they stepped in. Kamal reached across her to press the button and Rhea could have sworn she felt a crackle of static electricity leap between them. It startled her, her body's immediate, even primeval response to his closeness, the scent of him flooding her brain and turning off all circuitry that controlled rational behaviour.

She closed her eyes. Perhaps it was just the exhaustion of a very long day that made her feel like she couldn't stand on her feet any more. Or maybe, it was the shoes. She was not really accustomed to wearing very high heels for long periods at a stretch. Unthinkingly, she stepped out of her shoes and held them in her hand, transferring her tiny knot clutch rip-off to the other.

He looked bemused. 'Ah, now that feels better, doesn't it?'

She nodded and bent down to rub her feet where they were aching. He knelt down and took her foot in his hands, and gently kneaded the aching spot. She sucked a breath in and froze, unable to react at the oddly intimate gesture, and then felt her body turn to complete mush as his hands worked gently, surely, compelling her to put a hand on his shoulder to balance herself. He looked up at her and for a long moment they stared at each other. She almost reached out to draw him up and twine herself around him when the elevator pinged to a halt. The moment dissipated. He stood up and smiled at her. 'Feeling better?' She nodded mutely, her heart racing and she trying to steady her breath, uncertain of how to respond.

'You have a skill for this, did you train as a masseur?' she asked tritely, suddenly guilty about the fact that she wasn't able to resist him.

He laughed. 'Let's just say I trained long and hard.'

His eyes held hers and she had no doubt what he meant. She could feel her heart thud insanely against her ribs.

Damn this man and damn the effect his touch had on her. She had never felt this way before, not with any man, not with Samir. Now she couldn't imagine going back to Samir and returning to the half-baked lovemaking she had with him when she knew how a mere touch from Kamal could set off minor explosions in the deepest, hidden parts of her body.

He led her out of the elevator and towards the deck with the only 24-hour pizzeria and Indian restaurant on board. They walked with an uneasy silence between them, a silence that was a swirling of awareness of each other's physical proximity.

It was only after she settled into a chair on the deck, her plate piled with pizza that Rhea realized she had forgotten her manners. After all, he had waited patiently during the entire process of getting Rina Maasi to the medical room and further until she regained consciousness and was declared out of danger.

'Thank you,' she began. 'It was a great help, you being there. I am not the most organized person in crisis situations. I panic easily and can't take decisions.' He paused briefly from shepherding the fork plied with food to his mouth.

'There's nothing to thank me for,' he replied and turned his attention back to the food. It was disconcerting, she realized, to be seated across a handsome man and know that he found the food more attractive than her. Wasn't it barely minutes ago that his hands were doing such wanton things to her feet that almost had her have a screaming orgasm in public?

'We took you away from dinner with your sister and your . . . friend,' Rhea continued nonetheless. She realized that this was perhaps the last time she would be alone with him and felt her heart sink. Just a day more and they would go their separate ways. She would head back to Delhi, to her little room and the looming question of Samir. Kamal would be off to Mumbai, with Sonia dangling from his arm like an exotic jewel.

'Oh, they'll survive without me,' Kamal responded, breaking her train of thoughts. 'I only hope Naina finished her meal quickly and went back to relieve the babysitter early. The kids can be quite a handful, especially if they are sleepy,' he raised both eyebrows in mock exasperation. Rhea had seen evidence first-hand. A little shudder escaped her. He noted it, quick on the uptake.

'Not very fond of kids, are you?'

'It isn't politically correct to say so in these times,' she replied, feeling emboldened by the stars twinkling in the black velvet sky above, the crisp, soothing ocean breeze, and the softness in his eyes. 'I still have nightmares from the time I was made to babysit a bunch of under-ten cousins and sobbing from the horror,' she laughed. He looked at her quizzically. 'You never know how things change once you have your own children. For instance, Naina. She was a total party girl, ran a mile from anything in diapers, could drink anyone under the table. But once she had kids, she changed completely and became a total hands-on mom. Even for this trip, she could have brought the nanny along, in fact I had insisted on it, but she didn't. She prefers to do everything for them herself—from bathing to feeding. Which is great actually, given we have a lot of help at home. So I'm sure you'll make a wonderful mother too.'

He gave her a long, searching look. Why had Samir never given her these looks? Oh yes, those were reserved for his gadgets, the phone and the laptop.

'You seem tired. Or sad. Or perhaps both,' he said in a gentle voice and reached across the table to take her hand. His fingers toyed with the cameo ring on her finger. She had forgotten to ask the room steward where it had come from, she realized. It was probably Rina Maasi pulling a fast one on her, she wouldn't put it past her. His hand was firm, warm, she was tempted to lift it to her face, to have it stroke her cheek.

She looked down at her plate, noticing that she did not have any more appetite. It was so easy to let his hand hold hers, to let his lips seek hers, to let him mould her against his body . . . then she pulled her hand back.

'I wanted to talk to you about what Sonia said,' he said. 'I . . .'

But Rhea stopped him, despite wanting to hear what he had to say. She had to say what was on her mind first, say it before she was tempted to decide against it.

'Samir called. He messaged. He wants me back. Rina Maasi thinks it would be a good idea for me to go back to him too. My family would want me to get back with him and marry him.'

His eyes shuttered down. When he looked up at her again, his expression was haunted.

'And you,' he asked. 'What do you want?'

'I'm going to go back home and marry him. This . . .' she gestured vaguely at the two of them, '. . . should never have happened. It was a mistake, a terrible mistake.'

He placed both his hands on the table in an oddly supplicating gesture. 'Is that what you think about us, a terrible mistake?'

'Yes. It was a mistake. I will go back and marry Samir. It is what I should do. It is the most sensible thing to do,' she replied looking into her plate, not daring to look up and into his eyes, knowing that if she did, she might just melt and pull him to her. Then it would all be over—her self-respect, her bravado, and she would end up, as she feared, just another notch on his belt of sexual conquests.

The memories of his hands on her back, rubbing in the sun block with slow sensual strokes, the kisses they had exchanged, frantic, desperate, hovering delicately on the edge of complete surrender, the gentle kiss he placed on her forehead when he thought she was asleep, him taking her to a place she wanted to visit, watching out for her when she was drunk and dancing with John. Everything flashed before Rhea's eyes in glorious technicolour.

They sat there silently. Eventually Rhea decided to break it.

'It has been a long day. I think I should turn in now,' she said.

'You should,' he replied with a tired sigh.

They rose from their chairs and began walking towards the elevators. The decks were fairly deserted at this hour and there was no sound except the ship's as it cut through the ocean at a gentle pace, ensuring that even the queasiest of stomachs resisted sea sickness. The faint glow of a distant dawn gleamed over the horizon as they surged ahead on the black carpet of water below, dappled with the reflections of the stars and the lights from the ship.

'Goodbye Kamal,' she said, feeling a lump in her throat. 'I don't think we will be seeing each other again.'

He looked at her for a never ending moment. Her knees quavered unseemingly. She gulped, wondering what was coming next.

'Goodbye, Rhea,' he said, his tone painstakingly formal, 'It was nice meeting you on this cruise.'

'And thank you once again for helping with Rina Maasi last night,' she said, reluctant to see him go.

'It was my *guru dakshina*. I owed it to my teacher and the least I could do. If you need any help, you know my cabin number.'

And with that, he escorted her to the elevator bank, pressed her deck button and stood back, watching her enter and the glass doors close between them. At that moment Rhea realized that perhaps he wasn't the playboy Sonia portrayed him as. He was a gentle, caring soul who put family and the people he loved first. She had seen enough evidence to prove that—the fact that he had brought his sister and her children on the cruise, the unending patience with which he handled the kids, the way he watched out for his sister and for her when they had had a drink too many. And then last night when her aunt had an emergency, the way he rushed to help and not moved until the doctor sounded the all-clear bell. It struck her like a bolt. That look in his eyes as he let her go—she had misjudged him! In fact she had been misjudging him all through the trip! And now, she realized with a sinking heart, she would never see him again, would never be able to let him know how sorry she was for thinking wrongly of him.

FIFTEEN

Rhea woke up disoriented. Then she realized. The ship had docked when she was still asleep, and so when she woke up she was enveloped in a cacophony of different sounds—hooters blowing, voices calling, cars honking, basically everything that reminded her of being back on land and far away from the hushed serenity of the ocean.

She showered and changed into a pair of shorts, T-shirt, and a pair of sturdy sneakers and went to the infirmary. She had completed their packing in the early hours of the morning and except their hand baggage, all their luggage had been placed outside the cabin for clearing.

Rina Maasi, her face cleansed of all the make-up suddenly looked much older than she had seemed the previous evening. She was wide awake and flirting heartily with the male nurse who was administering her morning dose of medicine. She was definitely on the path to recovery! 'Have you brought my lipstick and a change of clothes?' she asked Rhea with the definite panic of one who feels naked without her lipstick. Rhea laughed and shook her head to indicate a no. 'Really Rina Maasi, the last thing you need to be bothered about right now is your lipstick. Let's get you back to the cabin and dressed to disembark.'

Maasi harrumphed. 'I'm scaring these poor innocent young lads here with this zombie face.'

'Don't you worry, Maasi, I'm sure they've seen much worse,' Rhea turned to ask the medical assistant, whose little badge announced him as a Steve. 'Haven't you, Steve?'

'Ma'am, you look gorgeous,' he said gallantly. 'Good looks run in the family it would seem.' He turned to Rhea and winked mischievously. She in turn couldn't help but smile back. It was endearing—the good humour with which men flirted outrageously on the ship, be it the crew or the passengers.

'How long are they planning to keep me locked up in this cave, Rhea? Don't we have to get off the ship in a couple of hours?'

'I need to check with the doctor, Maasi. Haven't met him yet,' she replied. 'But be glad that it wasn't anything worse. We could have been in serious trouble if this had happened in the middle of nowhere.'

'Actually, I couldn't think of a better way to go—in the middle of the ocean, with the sea below and the sky above. And none of the family around to make a song and dance about it. When I die, I want a burial at sea. Just tip the plank and have the fish eat me.' This was a change from her last request which had her declare she wanted her ashes scattered over the sand dunes in Rajasthan after a trip to the desert where she had fallen in love with the grandeur of the desolation. But then, that was Rina Maasi, always one for the dramatic gesture.

'Stop all this talk of burials and dying, Maasi, you're going to be fine and we're going ballroom dancing once you're out of here.'

Having got the all-clear from the good doctor a little later, Rina Maasi was taken to the cabin by a wheelchair despite her vociferous protests that she was not an invalid. They had a long day ahead and Rhea was already tired and groggy from the lack of adequate sleep. The final bill had to be settled, the luggage had probably been sent out already and was waiting for them to claim it on the pier, customs and immigration would need to be cleared again because they were re-entering Italy, and disembarking began at around 8.30 a.m. still a good one hour away. The arrangements had been told to them in advance. Their deck would be called and for those who were booked in the hotel for the day, there would be the hotel's bus awaiting. Others who had a connecting flight and had to go directly to the airport were to get into a different bus. There were of course some cruisers who would have private taxis awaiting them in order to take them to the airport or the hotel as their itinerary may be. For a brief second she wondered whether Kamal and Naina would be staying back in Rome for the day or would fly out to Mumbai the same day. If he wanted to track her down, he could always find Rina Maasi, and from there, she was but a phone call away. If he wanted to, that is.

But Rhea had made herself very clear. She was going home and going to marry Samir. To emphasize her decision to herself, she pulled out her phone and typed out a message to Samir. 'Back in Delhi in two days. Let's meet.' She received an immediate flood of replies, which should have made her soul soar with their unabashed declarations of devotion and undying love, but all they did was to make her terrified, yet again, about what she was getting herself into.

She was ready to get back to life as she knew it. Now all she needed to do was to exorcise the memories of the time she spent with Kamal which would be easier with the distance between Delhi and Mumbai, she told herself.

The Colonel arrived at their cabin and offered to wheel Rina Maasi to the queue if she felt weak. She shushed him and insisted on walking all the way. 'I'm not going to cop it so soon, Singhie. You're not going to be rid of me so easily,' she glowered. He laughed at her and kissed her cheek affectionately, nonetheless insisting she sit in the wheelchair rather than overexert herself.

Rhea began gathering up their things and wondered yet again who had placed that box with the ring on her bedside table. The cabin steward entered to say his goodbyes, and to receive, hopefully, an envelope conveying their appreciation of the service rendered.

'I wanted to ask you,' Rhea said, holding up the red velvet box which had contained the ring she was now wearing, 'if you knew how this box came to be by my bedside.'

He looked at it in surprise. 'No madam,' he said, 'I don't remember seeing this before.'

'Let it be,' said Rina Maasi. 'It's a pretty ring and you wanted it. Now you have it. How does it matter how it came to be by your bedside?'

'Of course, I'm bothered. Rings don't just appear, do they?'

Rina Maasi gave her a raised eyebrow look. 'So it is probably from an admirer who knew you wanted it. If the admirer chooses to stay anonymous, let him.'

'But it is very expensive! I can't take something so expensive from someone I don't know.'

'Oho, child. Just enjoy wearing it.'

This only confirmed Rhea's suspicions that her aunt had bought it for her and was not owning up for whatever vague reason she might have. Perhaps this was Rina Maasi's way of trying to make Rhea feel better about not being able to shop at all for herself.

They went onto the deck for breakfast and Rhea kept peering around hoping against hope that she would spot Kamal and Naina with the kids. She had, she admitted to herself in the most grudging manner, grown rather fond of Jay and Kiara, and would have liked to say goodbye to Naina. Perhaps she could call their cabin but on second thoughts decided against it.

Having finished their breakfast and completing the billing formalities with much agonizing over the charges for the medical treatment, they moved towards disembarking. On an impulse she called home, knowing it would mean a small ransom on her mobile bill for the next month but unable to contain an overwhelming urge to hear her mother's voice. Moreover she had to tell them that Rina Maasi had been taken ill on board.

'Rhea!' her mother's voice beamed. 'You haven't called for days, I hope you and Rina are fine.'

Rhea quickly filled her in with what had happened the previous evening, downplaying most of it, and insisting Rina Maasi was now perfectly fine.

'Samir came home,' her mother said. She had been expecting it. 'He's sorry, genuinely sorry for having run off like that. You must forgive him and take him back.'

'Ma,' she began, searching for words to tell her mother that she wasn't sure she loved Samir anymore and that a lot had changed in the past few weeks she had been away. But she didn't know where to start. 'He messaged me, called me. I'm confused. I know it is the sensible thing to do but I feel I don't love him anymore.'

There was a pregnant pause. A pin could have caused an explosion had it cared to drop now. Her father came on the line in a swift manner that could only mean her parents had her call on speaker phone.

'What nonsense are you talking about, Rhea? You went around with this man for years! You would have been married to him if it hadn't been for some foolishness on his part. Let me tell you, all men get terrified about getting married. If it hadn't been for the fear of my own father, I might have run away from my own wedding.'

'But Papa . . .' she tried to cut in without much success. Her father was in full flow and could not be interrupted. His voice had reached octaves of trembling anger. It was a good thing, she thought, that she could hold the receiver away from her ear and prevent ear drum damage.

'Now listen to me, Rhea,' he said, his voice clipped and angry. 'You will come back to India, you will tell Samir you will marry him and you will get married to him. Your mother and I are old now, and we want to see you settled before we die. There will be no further discussion about this.'

She disconnected the call quickly, her body shaking with rage. Speaking with her father without her mother to buffer the conversation always did this to her.

How dare he dictate what she should do with her life? Whose side was he on anyway—hers or Samir's? And she wasn't even a financial burden on them, if that is what his worry was. She was quite capable of earning her own living. She would be damned, she decided, if she got married to Samir just because her father wanted her to.

Rhea couldn't bear the thought of going home, not after the conversation with her parents. Samir would ring the doorbell, expecting her to open the door and welcome him with a warm embrace of forgiveness and a Come Back All Is Forgiven flag waving from the balcony. To make things worse, her parents expected her to wave that flag with enthusiasm. Mulling over the depressing thoughts, Rhea and Rina Maasi, along with the rest, moved towards the disembarkation point. Rhea felt as if she was letting something precious slip away, something she would never find again for the rest of her life even if she tried. Her heart sank.

The queue was inching forward, the morning was beginning to get hot, and she could feel damp patches begin to form in her armpits. She looked behind, on a hope and a prayer, trying to spot Kamal for one last time.

'I swear I won't speak a word to him, God, please, please, please . . .' she prayed hard.

Nada. Zilch. The area was buzzing with passengers from all over the world, all set to get off the Aqua Princess and get on with their journeys back home. But there was no sight of Kamal. Her heart sank further.

They were asked to wait in a lounge until their turn came and Rina Maasi sat happily on a sofa, chatting with the Colonel. Rhea stood against a wall, blinking back tears, pretending to examine a work of art that hung from the wall which was just a mash of motley colours swirling into the tears that she was mopping up before they brimmed over.

Just then, as they were called to move ahead, Rhea heard a familiar voice pipe up, a child's voice. She turned around. Naina, Kamal and the kids were just about taking their place in the fledgling queue being formed for their deck. Sonia was nowhere to be seen.

Naina spotted her, waved frantically and began walking across to meet her. Kamal, Rhea noted, looked at her, smiled politely and then looked pointedly away, his jaw square and gritted, looking heartbreakingly handsome in a baby blue shirt and faded denims. Rhea sighed and looked away from him.

'I wanted to speak with you before we left. I heard about the conversation between Sonia and you and realized I must have created some misunderstanding inadvertently.'

Rhea felt her stomach go queasy on her and gripped Naina's forearm to steady herself.

'How did you get to know about that?'

'From my brother, of course. Sonia is the daughter of old family friends of our parents, we have a common circle of friends and we've known each other for a while, but it was only recently that Kamal and Sonia began seeing each other . . . perhaps a few months ago.'

'But I was under the impression they were a long term couple?'

'I'm sorry, I just had to clarify this, they were seeing each other off and on, and dating for a few months. Of course, we all hoped they would get married, but they had a fallout and while I didn't know the details earlier, Kamal told me all about it last night and I understood why he could never marry her. But let me not get into that. That is something, if it needs telling, needs to be told by him.'

Rhea looked again in the distance, where Kamal was standing with the children, Kiara by his side and Jay on his shoulders. This time he looked straight at her and she felt her insides melt into mush instantly.

'Why are you telling me this, Naina?' she asked. 'What does this have to do with me?'

Naina took a deep breath and continued, 'I think my brother has grown terribly fond of you over the past couple of weeks. And I've never seen him so concerned, so keen about any girl in the past. I hope you did realize he was trying his best to woo you, in his own rather awkward way. When he told me about what Sonia said to you, I thought I needed to clear things up.'

She sighed.

'Sonia had no business calling you a social climber and she had no business at all telling you to stay away from Kamal because she's making a last ditch attempt to woo him back when he's least interested in any relationship with her.'

Rhea ran a hand over her forehead, trying to figure out what it was that Naina was actually trying to tell her.

'Kamal told Sonia off in my presence last evening about the way she spoke to you. Especially after what he had learnt about her. Sonia was amongst the first to disembark this morning. He told her that he didn't want to see her ever again and to stop deluding herself that he was serious about a relationship with her.'

'What you're saying, Naina, is that they were seeing each for a few months and they split because of something so nasty you can't bear to tell it to me?'

Naina nodded grimly. 'That's my brother, he's very old school about not bandying a woman's name in disrespectful terms, though if I were in his place I would be hard pressed to even be civil with Sonia. She's a total . . .' her voice trailed off and she looked guiltily at Kamal in the off chance that her voice had carried over the distance.

'Now though, it is completely up to you. God knows, my brother is besotted with you. You're all he can talk about. And you must like him a bit too, if you're wearing the ring he bought you.'

She lifted Rhea's hand up and the coral cameo glistened in the bright Mediterranean sunlight, the lady within catching fire from the rays of the morning sun. 'Kamal bought this?' Rhea's jaw fell. 'I didn't know it was him. How did he know I liked it?'

'I think he was right behind us in the shop when you tried it on. He bought it for you and then didn't have the courage to give it to you directly so he tipped your cabin steward to keep it by your bedside, without telling who it was from.'

Rhea looked at Kamal again. He was looking right back at her with a strange expectancy she couldn't quite comprehend, and then, in that moment, all the decisions were made. All the doubts clouding her mind were gone, just like a brisk shower clears the sky and makes the sunlight clearer.

She dropped the little overnighter in her hand down and hugged Naina. 'Thank you Naina, thank you so much. You don't know just how much I owe you.'

With that Rhea took off towards Kamal, her feet barely touching the ground in her haste to get to him. His eyes widened in surprise. The world around them slowed down as he set Jay down and reached out to put his arms around her as she dashed into him, the speed making her unable to contain the impact. And then Rhea, without a moment's hesitation and without a care of being in public, pulled his face down to hers and kissed him passionately. When they finally broke for air, she was vaguely conscious of around a hundred pairs of eyes on them, some approving, others disapproving. She drew back a step, only to find Kamal pulling her back firmly against him, his mouth seeking hers out again for a kiss so deep, so passionate, her entire body trembled in response.

They stopped and looked into each other's eyes, unmindful of the entire queue staring at them. His voice, when he finally broke the silence between the two of them, was husky, whether with emotion or a bad throat, she did not know. 'This is not a terrible mistake, is it Rhea?'

She shook her head. 'No, not a mistake.'

Despite herself and the innumerable censorious eyes on them, she drew his head down to hers again and kissed him again, surely, tenderly and confidently.

'I'm sorry,' she said, 'I've been really silly and prickly, and assuming the worst of you when you gave me absolutely no reason to. I apologize.'

'Apology accepted. And now I have something to say to you,' he put her hand up to his lips, kissed it, and gently pulled off the cameo ring she had worn on her right hand. 'You have worn this on the wrong finger on the wrong hand, you doofus. It needs to go here.'

He lifted her left hand and placed the ring gently on the tip of her ring finger, and looked at her as she looked at him, startled with what the gesture implied. Her breath caught in her throat as she realized what he was trying to say. 'It might seem a bit too soon, Rhea Khanna, given I've barely met you a couple of weeks ago, but I feel I've known you for years, and have been waiting for you all my life. I've never been surer of anything in my life. Will you marry me?' He wasn't kneeling down, looking up into her eyes, it wasn't a candlelight dinner at a fancy restaurant, and she hadn't spent the day defoliating, tweezing, buffing herself for the moment. But it was a story she could tell their grandchildren, the story of how their grandfather proposed to her moments before they were to get off a cruise ship and lose each other forever.

There was a slight tug on the hem of her shorts and a piping voice commanded sharply, 'Say yes.' A sharper, older female voice from behind her, which she recognized as Rina Maasi's, seconded the command issued from the child. 'Go on, say yes.'

'Is this a conspiracy?' she laughed, looking back to see Rina Maasi, the Colonel and Naina all standing a few paces away, watching them, their faces expectant and excited.

She looked down at Jay scowling up at her, his grip still threateningly firm on her shorts, laughed and nodded a 'yes' to Kamal. 'Yes, yes, yes, I will marry you, Kamal, I will,' she laughed through her tears. And with that he slid the ring on her finger, kissed her again and again until she was breathless and had to rest her head on his shoulder to steady her heart, and the spontaneous applause that broke out around them was sweeter than any music she had ever heard.

ACKNOWLEDGEMENTS

With *All Aboard!* I take the deep plunge into the rose-tinted world of romance writing which has been quite an adventure for me to say the very least—me being old, cynical, embittered and, as Plum Wodehouse would say, a twenty-minute hard-boiled egg.

I'd like to, therefore, thank the very fabulous Vaishali Mathur, senior commissioning editor at Penguin Random House, who believed I had a true blue romance tucked away somewhere below my cynical carapace and didn't give up on me, hand holding me through this entire book with infinite patience, much more than I deserved. Many thanks due to editors Paloma Dutta and Azera Rahman, as well. Because I am such a sucker for lovely covers, a huge thank you to Tara Upadhyay for the fabulous work.

From the bottom of my cholesterol-laden heart, infinite gratitude to my darling Tisca Chopra, who is a living embodiment of how it is completely possible to be beautiful on the inside and outside, and to the fabulous, effervescent and ever-smiling Tara Sharma Saluja, who has been so generous with her support, always.

Thank you to my wonderful family—my mother, Shama Sheikh, for putting up with me while growing up when I always had my nose in a book, any book, to escape from learning any useful taxable and non-taxable life skills. Thank you to my sisters-in-law Pramila, Chanda and Tara for indulging me, pampering me and making me their youngest sister. Thank you to my mother-in-law Leela Manral for allowing me the luxury of not having to worry about domestic chaos and get on with my writing. And to my darling son, Krish, for being the dynamite under my short fuse every single day.

And finally—thank you to my husband, Kirit, who will always remain to me the unsure and terribly gorgeous boy I had met in the January of 1991 who took my breath away. Thank you for always being my knight in shining armour, albeit a bit creaky at the joints now.